Katharine Davies

THE MADNESS OF LOVE

VINTAGE

First published in Great Britain in 2004
with the title A Good Forger by

Random House, 20 Vauxhall Bridge Road,
London SW1V 2SA

Random House Australia (Pty) Limited
20 Alfred Street, Milsons Point, Sydney,
New South Wales 2061, Australia

Random House New Zealand Limited
18 Poland Road, Glenfield,
Auckland 10, New Zealand

Random House (Pty) Limited
Endulini, 5A Jubilee Road, Parktown 2193,
South Africa

The Random House Group Limited Reg. No. 954009
www.randomhouse.co.uk/vintage

A CIP catalogue record for this book
is available from the British Library

ISBN 0 099 46843 5

Papers used by Random House are natural, recyclable products made from wood grown in sustainable forests. The manufacturing processes conform to the environmental regulations of the country of origin

Printed and bound in Great Britain by
Cox & Wyman Limited, Reading, Berkshire

Now the melancholy god protect thee, and the tailor make thy doublet of changeable taffeta, for thy mind is a very opal. I would have men of such constancy put to sea, that their business might be everything, and their intent everywhere, for that's it that always makes a good voyage of nothing.

Twelfth Night, II.iv

1

MELODY

He walked into the wind, his back to the inland sky,
oblivious of the snow that was at that moment about
to fall and that then fell on Illerwick. He looked
only outwards, across the waves, ignoring the yellow
eyes of the sheep that lined his way and lifted their
heads to watch his passing. His hands swung bravely
by his sides, as in a march. At the end of the head-
land he stopped and allowed the wind to sweep away
all his thoughts. He listened to the sea's slow breaths
and echoed them with his own and this calmed him.
There was a boom, far below, like a drum roll. The
seagulls cried in encouragement. He crouched
down, his thighs taut, his bitten nails buried in the
wet grass. There was not a false start. He took a
run at it, towards the air. He did not keep running,
cartoonishly, only to hover and look down in fear.
He executed a perfect dive and fell, like a stone,
into immediate nothing.

This is what Melody imagined afterwards, when
they told her what had happened to Gabriel. She
thought, it's what he would have wanted.

2
FITCH

Miss Vye was standing with her back to the window when Fitch and the others came in. The great height of the window made her look smaller than she really was. Outside, the snow made the light bright. It hurt Fitch's eyes to look at Miss Vye against that particular light but when he closed them her miniature silhouette was tattooed on the inside of his eyelids. He opened them. He couldn't see the expression on her face. He wondered if she had only just turned round or if she had been watching him in line as he came in from the playground. She moved to the blackboard, smoothing her dress over her hips, and was tall again. She seemed to be studying something on her desk as she waited for them to grow calm. The noise of voices lessened as she started to take the register silently, her sea-green eyes flicking up to each face, her lips moving slightly as she said their names under her breath. He watched her teeth release her lower lip on the whispered 'F' of his name. His heart was beating. He said her name inside his head: Melody.

The class was quieter than usual, exhausted by

the snow. Miss Vye looked at the class and into Fitch's eyes but he looked down, his face burning. The talking stopped; they had known her for four years so no one could be bothered to disobey her. She seemed about to speak but then she turned to the blackboard. Fitch felt relief wash over him. He pressed his forehead down onto the pile of books on his desk. When he looked up he felt dazed. He saw that his head had left a greasy, heart-shaped stain on the front of his English book. He turned it over. A ruler was digging into his arm. Suzy passed him a square of paper folded about a million times but he knew what it said without reading it. He ate it. A question was appearing on the board in Miss Vye's italic hand. Miss Vye sneezed as she always did when she wrote on the blackboard and the sneeze made her forget the question mark but there was no doubt that what she had written was a question. It was about the madness of love in the play and it contained the word 'topsy-turvydom'. It was now up to them to answer the question. Miss Vye was writing some instructions. Fitch read the words over and over again but they seemed to make no sense. He put up his hand.

'Yes?' She smiled at him. It was the last time she would smile for weeks but no one knew that yet.

'Miss Vye . . .' He forgot what he wanted to ask. He went red. There were some titters.

Dave's voice came from the back of the class: 'You've forgotten the question mark, Miss.'

Miss Vye added the question mark without saying anything. Fitch could see Dave's face smirking without needing to look. Dave's parents ran the newsagent's and he thought friendship could be bought in exchange for sweets.

Everyone else had started. The clock got louder. Fat Pete farted twice. But outside it had started to snow again and Fitch found it hard not to look out of the window at the whiteness, hard not to just sit and watch the accretion of snow on the trees. Suzy sighed dreamily, her squat letters filling the lines. Fitch wrote the title at the top of the page then he wrote the date, January 5th, in the margin in the left hand corner. He started with a quotation. Miss Vye always told them to weave quotations into their sentences. Miss Vye said his writing was spidery. He tried to disguise its spideriness by making it italic but it only got more spidery. He looked up. Miss Vye seemed to be staring at him. She began to walk up the narrow aisle between the desks towards him, glancing at the essays in other people's books as she came. She bent over his desk and a coil of her flame-coloured hair fell against his ear. He had an erection. She moved away. A gritting lorry was rumbling down the road and a man called Leo Spring, who was going to start teaching him the piano soon, was walking past the school railings wearing a Russian hat. Leo Spring's face turned once, quickly and blindly, in the direction of the classroom and then stared fixedly ahead but Miss Vye had suddenly dropped her book and was at that moment bending down to pick it up so she didn't see him. She went back to her desk on the side of the room furthest from the window, sidestepping her way around Pete's broad back.

Fitch became absorbed in his essay. He had written one and a half pages of his exercise book and woven in eighteen quotations when there was a knock at the door. He stopped writing. A few people almost stood up as Mr Boase, the deputy headmaster, edged into the room but he gestured for them to sit. He went and whispered something in the ear of Miss Vye. She made a small noise in the back of her throat. No one was writing now. They watched her go pale. She started to gather the papers from her desk but Mr Boase put a restraining hand on her arm. She left the papers. She turned away and faced the wall. Mr Boase put his arm briefly around her shoulder. Fitch hated him; anyone else would have spoken to her outside. Miss Vye picked up her handbag and ran out.

Suzy looked at Fitch with wide eyes. The room began to fill with whispers but not the laughing kind. Mr Boase sidled to the front of the teacher's desk and said, 'Right!' but he had no presence. People had abandoned their essays now. Pete and Dave were leaning back in their chairs listening amicably to the girls in the row in front. The sound of voices was getting louder and when Suzy offered to collect the books, since it was only five minutes until home time, Mr Boase said, 'Very well.' Fitch saw that his book was on the top but now he wondered if Miss Vye would ever mark them. The bell rang and most of the others barged out. He left Suzy in the classroom trying to wheedle out of Mr Boase what was wrong with Miss Vye. He didn't speak to anyone. He lingered in the corridor. Mr

Boase would not tell her. He waited in the boys' cloakroom so that Suzy would think he'd gone. He didn't speak to anyone. The snow was falling faster and a group of boys was running up the playing field hurling snowballs. He turned sharply left out of the school gates and walked along Broad Street past a boy in the year below who asked him if he was going sledging down Bryn Mawr.

He said, 'Maybe later.'

He kept walking. He knew where he was going. He had travelled this distance in his dreams for weeks. He crossed the river. It looked black and shiny in the fading light. He was only wearing his blazer but the snow just seemed to tickle him. He felt exhilarated. The tune of a film he had watched the night before swooped through his mind. When he got to Miss Vye's house it was in darkness. There were no tracks that he could see. He leaned against her front door. Everything was silent because of the snow. He saw a light through the trees. He went towards it. He walked through the snow, through the woods, along the edges of fields and crept into a garden. It was like a garden in a dream. He looked in at the windows of the house of Leo Spring. Leo Spring was sitting in a red velvet armchair smoking. He looked as though he might be listening to music. He stubbed out his cigarette and put his head, with the Russian hat still on it, in his hands. His body started to rock backwards and forwards. A terrible sobbing noise reached Fitch through the glass. He ran all the way home, snow soaking through his school shoes.

3

VALENTINA

The morning rush hour surged around them but they were separate from it. They pressed their heads together then they let go. They backed away from each other slowly, out of syncopation with the hurrying waves of movement on either side, lifting their hands simultaneously in a gesture of farewell. In Jonathan's face, Valentina saw a reflection of her own. He turned on his heel and was carried away in a sea of people but Valentina knew he would look back and he did. He gave a last, high wave, his arm rising above the mass of heads like a mast as his scarlet jacket moved through the crowds. Then he was swallowed up. She stood still and the crowds flowed into the gap he had left behind him. She looked up at the vault of air above her. She closed her eyes and heard only the soft shuffling of thousands of feet. When she opened her eyes, a lost seagull was wheeling about and she watched it fly out through an arch. Then she made a decision and her life took an entirely new course.

The hairdresser's was called Babushka's. It was ten past nine in the morning but inside there was a permanent evening of darkness and gloom. Behind a high counter a sleepy girl was doodling. Valentina waited for the girl to focus on her. She stood limply while a plastic cape was fastened round her neck, then the girl led her into a side room and told her to wait. Cold light streamed in through a narrow window in the back wall. Everything was blue and gold and the walls were lined with ornate dressing tables decorated with real seashells and sprinklings of sand. The scissors and brushes and combs lay in their positions. Valentina sat down and faced herself in the mirror.

If she took the band off the end of her plait and shook out her hair, it would spread out like a golden cloak and fall down the sides of the chair, the growth of years of her life. When she was a young child her mother used to cut half an inch off once in a blue moon, murmuring the words, 'Such beautiful hair, such beautiful hair . . .' like a mantra. She told her that Sri Lankan women did not cut their hair until they were married and Valentina had dreaded the thought of marrying if it meant cutting her hair. Jonathan's hair was cut regularly. It was because he was a boy. Sometimes she thought he was envious of her hair but she had never been envious of his. When she knelt on the sand at Tangalla with the sea-wind drying hers, she liked to imagine that she was the Little Mermaid.

She remembered her mother's long black hair, like treacle. Once, she had it cut to her shoulders and Valentina had told her she looked like a witch. She remembered her father, once, gently combing out her own hair after it had been washed. She remembered sitting on the verandah with Jonathan on the evening of their thirteenth birthday, passing their fingers through candle flames, moths settling on their wrists. That night they had been called to their father's room because he was dying. She remembered the papery feel of her father's moley skin against her lips, the billowing of the mosquito net in the fan, the fear of what was happening. They sat on the roof all night, under an enormous moon, with the music of insects all around them, clinging to each other while their father died in the room below and they realised they were becoming orphans.

She thought of Jonathan, now a man, standing on the beach at Tangalla, the air and light all around him, the ocean crashing at his feet, and hated him for saying he wanted to go back to Sri Lanka on his own, for breaking the promise that they would only go back together. Her hair felt like the terrible weight of his rejection. It was pulling her, dragging her down, and her fingers itched to pick up the sharpest pair of scissors on the dressing table and hack it off herself.

She had expected the hairdresser to undo her plait, to spread out her curtain of hair and cut it off bit by bit. She had imagined the curls settling like feathers around their feet until they were knee deep in hair. But the hairdresser didn't do that. She cut off her plait in one snip like Rapunzel's. Valentina screamed. The hairdresser laughed and pulled her back to the basin and when she got back to the mirror, she had the tousled head of a boy. She felt the cool air around her skull. Then the clipping started and went on until all she could see was her twin brother's face staring out of the mirror. She smiled his smile. She thought, my strength has not been taken away. Now I will have an adventure of my own.

4

FITCH

The day of Fitch's first piano lesson with Leo Spring had come and he was standing in the lane, waiting for the sound of his father's van to die away. The sky was an incredible cartoon blue. He opened the gate in the middle of a tall yew hedge and walked up the drive, the gravel underneath his trainers crunching too loudly, the windows of the house staring blackly at him as he made his way through the mottled garden. All around him were the jeers of crows as they gathered in the trees. He knocked and waited in the porch. There was a seat with a heart carved into its back. He almost sat in it. He thought he could hear hoovering inside. He thought about running home across the fields, the way he had come in the snow. Eventually, the door was opened, not by Leo Spring, but by Ellie Swales, who used to be a barmaid in The Crown. Fitch thought, perhaps he has forgotten, but Ellie said, 'He's in there,' and pointed to a door leading off the left side of the hall. She switched the hoover back on and dragged it away, cracking the flex like a whip.

Fitch did not move. He stood in the vastness of the hall on its chessboard floor and the face of Miss Vye flew into his mind. He thought, I am doing this for you. Slowly, he opened the door Ellie had pointed at and a wave of music rushed over him. He felt goose pimples on his thighs. Leo Spring was sitting, hatless, in his red, velvet armchair and it seemed that the wild spirals of his hair were tiny antennae picking up the notes. A wind-up gramophone was on the table before him and he was staring at the fire as if he thought he was keeping it ablaze with his eyes. There was a final chord. Fitch watched as Leo Spring wound up the gramophone without taking his eyes off the fire. There was a crackly pause before the music began again. Fitch shifted his weight from one foot to the other and his trainer made a squeaking noise on the polished floor. Leo Spring looked up, their eyes meeting quickly as the first flurry of notes began, then he looked back at the fire. He had the saddest eyes Fitch had ever seen. Fitch scanned the room in vain for a piano, not daring to leave his post by the door. A smell of soot hung in the air, as though the chimney needed sweeping. The music held them in its grip. Fitch watched the rabble of crows in the trees and tried to count them. He remembered the terrible sobbing sound. His insides fluttered. He bent down and pretended to tie his laces.

'Hello, Fitch,' said Leo, smiling a smile with just the right amount of teeth in it. 'Melody has told me all about you.'

Leo Spring's voice did not go with his spirals of

hair. Fitch had recently watched *Brief Encounter* on TV because Miss Vye had said it was her favourite film and Leo Spring's voice reminded him of Trevor Howard's. He could imagine how he would say 'darling'. 'Darling Melody. Melody, darling.' He tried not to imagine the possibility of these words in Leo Spring's mouth. He thought of Celia Johnson's husband sitting in an armchair while Rachmaninov surged in the background and he heard himself saying, 'Thank you for coming back to me.'

Leo Spring told Fitch to call him Leo. He clasped his cigarette case with his long fingers, flicking it open and offering it to Fitch before seeming to notice, as if for the first time, that Fitch was only a boy. Fitch thought, this man is not an ordinary person; his hair alone makes him unusual; another factor is his wind-up gramophone. He hated the thought that Miss Vye had called him her friend. He heard her words, 'A friend of mine could give you lessons, Fitch.' He thought of them laughing together. Her silvery laugh.

They went on a tour of the house because Leo said it was what people always wanted to do but never liked to ask. He walked quickly, almost running along the cold, dim corridors on his spindly legs and Fitch hurried after him, trying to keep a mental note of the number of rooms so he could tell his father, but after a while he lost count. All the rooms seemed dead anyway with their shrouded furniture and dust. There was only one room in which Leo lingered. The exotic birds and flowers, he said, had been painted on the walls a hundred years ago. The room looked out onto the old rose garden and had a four-poster bed in the middle of it with an embroidered coverlet. Leo drew back the long, blue curtains and leaned for a long time on the windowsill. He said the name for a flock of crows was a murder and Fitch, pretending that he did not already know this, said, 'Really?'

In the drawing room there was a grand piano with a shiny lid, like a black lake, and a harp. Leo sat down and softly began to play the music he had been listening to on the gramophone and Fitch thought, I have never seen anyone with such an expressive back, but then Leo stopped and went to the french windows.

'Now you,' he called over his shoulder.

Fitch sat down and studied the faded music on the stand. He noted the number of sharps and ledger lines. He felt the sweat roll down his arms inside his shirt. Pausing every so often to read the notes, he struggled through the piece until he got to the bottom of the page. Leo was standing behind him. Fitch waited for him to turn the page, half expecting him to give his shoulder a Trevor Howard squeeze.

'Good,' he said gently. 'Melody loves Beethoven, as I'm sure you know. I think that's enough for today.'

Fitch stared into his wide, pale eyes. He wanted to ask what was between him and Miss Vye, if it was Miss Vye who made him cry.

Suddenly, Leo said, 'It was her brother. He was drowned off Breakers Point.'

He plucked the sheet music from the stand and

gave it to Fitch. Fitch took it, not saying that he knew, not saying that it had been in all the papers.

That night, Fitch looked down on Illerwick from his attic bedroom at the top of Bryn Bach. He thought of Miss Vye alone now in her house by the river. He could not tell which were the lights of her house. He looked out towards the beech woods and saw the lights of Leo Spring's house shining like a beacon. He imagined him at a high window, looking out over his moonlit garden. He wanted to hate him.

For the next week he stayed behind after school every day and played the *Moonlight Sonata* in the dinner hall until Mr Boase told him to go home. He wanted her to walk in with a pile of books under her arm and see him. Sometimes he felt she was there as he played. He thought, she loves Beethoven and so do I and now her brother is drowned.

The funeral car went past one morning during Maths. Mr Boase told them to face the front. Fitch saw a crescent of her face beneath her hat's black veil.

5

VALENTINA

After her haircut, Valentina walked to work. She kept reaching up to her hair to stop it blowing in the wind and then realising that it wasn't there any more. But as she pushed open the shop door, her reflection in the black glass behind the gold copper-plate letters of 'LEAVES: *the bookshop for the green-fingered*' pleased her.

Valentina was on shelving duty when a man came into the shop. There were no other customers. Miss Bratby was out buying a cappuccino. The man was whistling as though he thought he shouldn't really have been there. He kept looking around anxiously. Eventually, he drifted over to the foot of Valentina's ladder so she asked him if she could help him.

'I don't know,' he said mournfully.

Valentina waited and as he didn't say anything else, she came down her ladder and said, 'Are you looking for anything in particular?' in the sort of shop voice that Miss Bratby encouraged.

'I have a vision . . .' he trailed off.

'Are you designing a garden?' she prompted.

'In a way. It's a project, you see. A Grand Scheme. A renovation.'

She led him towards the Design section. He followed with the air of someone who has no clue about anything, let alone the designing or even renovation of a garden.

Miss Bratby was back at the till so Valentina pulled out two wheelie stools and showed the man an array of books on knot gardens, old roses and even one on how to make your own maze. He immersed himself in the pictures for a while. Valentina thought she smelt a whiff of alcohol on his breath. He put his head in his hands and sighed.

'It's no use,' he said. 'I can't do this on my own. It is just not my forte. What I need is a gardener.'

And then an amazing thing happened.

Valentina said, 'I think I could help you there.'

He said, 'Oh?'

'I've got a degree in Horticulture,' she said, improbably.

He looked at her keenly. She considered her lie. At least it was only the subject she had changed, and English Literature was full of gardens.

She lowered her voice. 'This is just a temporary job to pay off my overdraft.' That part was true. 'They took me on because I know so much about plants. My real ambition is to be a garden designer.' That part wasn't.

The man did not question the likelihood of what she said. He smiled a devastating smile and said, 'Here's my card.'

It said: *Leo Spring*
          Beech House
          Illerwick

This is my new life beginning already, she thought. She watched him carry his stack of books to the till. Miss Bratby smiled at her around the side of his hair. Valentina felt sorry that she would have to tell Miss Bratby she was leaving. All day she dreamed of her new life-to-be as a gardener in Illerwick, wherever that was. She knew it was her hair that had swayed him. He could see that it wouldn't get tangled in the plants.

On the tube back to Finsbury Park that night, several things floated into her mind. One was Leo Spring's devastating smile. Another was Jonathan last night on Westminster Bridge in the rain saying he would go to Sri Lanka come hell or high water. Last of all, there was the green-painted desk in her bedroom that seemed like a little boat carrying the precious cargo of her real ambition, which she had told no one: to be a writer. On the way home, she went to Oxfam and bought a new journal with a red Chinese silk cover.

Now I will really have something to write about, she thought, as she looked up Illerwick in an atlas of the British Isles.

6
MELODY

Melody lay in hideous darkness. The curtains had been lined with old blankets in the days when the house had no central heating, and they let in not even a sliver of moonlight. Her throat ached with the longing to cry but what came from her mouth were not sobs but groans, like retches, and her eyes were dry as they blinked helplessly in the blackness. I am in an abyss, she thought.

Every hour she heard the church clock chime as though it were far away in the distance even though she could have walked there in five minutes. It chimed three. She pulled the eiderdown from the bed, trailed to the window with it wrapped around her and opened the curtain. She looked out across the moonlit fields and thought of the children she taught lying in their different beds all over the town.

'*Slowly, silently, now the moon*
Walks the night in her silver shoon,' she said softly.

Gabriel was lying in his grave in the new cemetery next to the bypass, the fresh earth on top of him like a heavy blanket. But then, she thought, it's not him any more. It's just his shell. She remembered a photograph of him on the beach grinning madly when she had buried him in sand. Snug as a bug in a rug. She thought of her parents lying side by side, as though in bed, in the church graveyard. She went back to bed. It felt like a grave. They had all slept in this bed at one time or another. First it was her parents' bed, and she and Gabriel would crawl into the heat of it with their mother while their father was up and shaving. Then it had become the sick-bed. When Gabriel had one of his asthma attacks he would lie there reading during the day, propped up by pillows, and a fire would be lit. The image of Gabriel with his nose in a book suddenly made her think of something. She got up, switched on the light and went downstairs to the hall where his duffel bag had lain untouched for two weeks. Shivering, she felt inside. She pulled out a book. She knew there were other things in there that she would have to look at eventually. She took the book upstairs and waited until she was in bed before opening it slowly. It was *Wuthering Heights*. She had given it to him for Christmas because he had said he'd never read it. The corner of a page was folded down and it was the thought that he would never finish it that made her cry for the first time.

In the morning Mary came over from The Crown to check on her. She took *Wuthering Heights* off the pillow and closed it. She gave her the letters of condolence she had found on the doormat. There was one from Leo Spring, which had been delivered by hand. In it he suggested that they meet. Melody wrote her reply immediately and asked Mary to post it. She thought: he must face facts.

7
JONATHAN

Jonathan looked out of the plane window at the quilted clouds. He didn't like flying. He never had, even when they were younger. He thought of their flight back to England from Colombo when they were thirteen, remembered the fear – a heavy thing in his stomach like an extra piece of luggage of which he was ashamed. Valentina wasn't afraid. She had pretended to be because she knew he was, but there had never been anything heavy inside her in spite of everything that had happened. He saw her as she had been then, leaning against the window, her long hair full of light, watching England getting closer, pointing at the chequered fields, pulling at his sleeve to make him look out of the window through the clouds and down through the air.

Now he was facing his fear, as he had a few times since then, and it was getting easier as the flight went on. Now he could look out across the rolling white mass and allow himself to think a little. He thought he could feel a new Jonathan emerging. He thought that perhaps he was becoming a man of the world, putting the money his parents had left him to a use which would make them proud. Perhaps one day, he would find a way of earning a living which meant that he would travel the globe as a matter of routine. He considered his luggage, the carefully planned contents of his rucksack, everything light, everything travel-sized: the mosquito net, the torch, the Swiss army knife he'd always wanted. No extras. It was not as if you couldn't buy most things in Sri Lanka, and he would be staying in people's houses from time to time so he didn't need all that much. But he liked the economy of it, the challenge of fitting everything in, the feeling of being prepared. It reminded him of when he went to boarding-school, before he found out how awful it was going to be. He thought, Valentina was not afraid then, either.

He saw Valentina's face last night, needled by rain and by shock when he'd told her about the trip. He knew he shouldn't have left it so late to tell her. He knew he had left it so late because he couldn't tell her. She said he was breaking the promise they had made to each other when they were thirteen, the day they left Colombo, at the airport. She remembered exactly where they had been standing she said, looking at the lined-up planes, at the dusty green palm trees. He said, what promise? He didn't remember until she told him last night, shouting in the middle of all the rain. Then he did remember. But it was too late. Everything was arranged, the ticket bought, his bags packed, his contract at Computer World terminated. She had said plans can always be undone if you really want to undo them. He had thought of his rucksack, the tightly packed pockets, the malaria pills he'd already started taking. He thought of himself standing on Galle Face Green. He shouted back, but it had got suddenly quieter and his words seemed grandiose. Come hell or high water was what he had said, because he had been a little drunk, full of his last taste of a real pub and of the taste for a single-handed adventure.

She said they'd never been this far apart, not in different countries. Never for so long. He had said, things change. They have to change. But he knew that she was thinking of that night when everything changed under the moon.

Now a trick of the light in the double-layered window seemed to project a faint version of himself out into the white unknown territory of the clouds. He felt the distance between himself and Valentina opening up. The flat they shared in Finsbury Park was far away now. He thought of Valentina at work in Leaves and an image came to him of himself returning from his trip and going to find her there, of how he would come up behind her and tug the long bell-pull of her plait and she would turn around and he would tell her about all the things that were still to come and she would change her mind and see the sense in this solo voyage of rediscovery.

8
VALENTINA

Valentina sat rigidly in the cold, empty train compartment, scrunching up her toes inside her boots in an effort to warm them. The white fields unfolding and unfolding reminded her of the blank pages of the journal in her suitcase. In her mind, she described the frost-thickened cobwebs among the hedge twigs, the inky spattering of ravens around a dead sheep, the black veins of the trees against the fleshy sky. She tried to imagine herself transcribing these images onto the first page of her journal, sitting propped up in a new bed in a new room, but found that she could not. It was too unknown. What came to her were other beds in other rooms. What came to her was the past in another country. And because of this and because there was no more light and only her strange, short-haired reflection to look at, she took a book on garden design from her bag and projected her thoughts to the end of winter. To her future life, whatever that might be.

She spread out Leo Spring's crinkled, hand-drawn plan of the gardens of Beech House which he had sent her the previous week and studied its squares of lawn, its oblong of kitchen garden and its segmented rose beds. She closed her eyes and filled the empty spaces with hedges of lavender and box, honeysuckle and clematis arches and herbaceous borders full of delphiniums and hollyhocks – romantic pictures she had seen in the bookshop. But Leo Spring had described it as a wilderness in his letter. What she had imagined could only evolve slowly. It was a lifetime's work and yet how long did she really plan to stay? And more to the point, what did she really know about gardening? She opened her eyes. For an instant, her reflection became Jonathan's face at a Sri Lankan train window. He looked straight through her.

Leo Spring's letter had instructed her go to the cab office opposite the station. It smelt of fag butts and grease and a listless boy was playing on a machine in the corner. A pair of enormous women, eating chips behind the glass partition, looked surprised when she said her destination was Illerwick.

'Take 'bout forty minutes,' one of them said sceptically.

'That'll be a job for Sid,' smirked the other.

After a wait of ten minutes, an old estate car drew up and she got into it, hauling her case in beside her since the driver remained wedged into his fake-furred seat. He fiddled with the cassette player with one hand and swung them round the town's one-way system with the other. A few bedraggled Christmas decorations flailed infelicitously in the wind. Then they were hurtling along pitch-black minor roads at seventy miles an hour to the tragic yodelling of Patsy Cline and it felt as though she were being rushed towards the ends of the earth. Eventually, her eyes grew accustomed to a darkness softened by moonlight glancing off the snowy landscape. She could feel the driver's eyes darting at her in the mirror, wondering, building up to a barrage of questions. She wished he would keep his eyes on the road and that he would slow down. She gripped the fake-fur seat like a mane.

'Come from London . . . ? Holiday . . . ? Running away . . . ?' A rueful laugh as though he knew all about that.

But maybe because it was dark, and because she felt afraid and alone, she answered his questions in a way that she would normally have not. She told him that she was going to work for a man called Leo Spring about whom she knew almost nothing and she told him that she was only a pseudo garden designer. It felt as though he were the last person on the shore of her old world.

'Knowed him from when I was a boy,' he said, turning down 'Crazy'. 'My dad did a job over there on the roof. Odd. Load of old hippies up at that house.'

'Not too odd, I hope.' Her own voice sounded pompous in the furry darkness.

'Just a few rumours.'

And then she told him about Jonathan going away and the breaking of their promise.

'It will all come out in the wash,' he said as, at

27

last, he began to drive more slowly along an ungritted lane where there was still a layer of hard snow. In the distance, the outlandish shape of a large building loomed. Her heart thudded. What madness had brought her here?

There were no automatic lights in the courtyard of Beech House. As she paid the driver, she suddenly felt that she didn't want him to go. He gave her the printed card of the taxi firm and it felt like a talisman; whatever happened, she could always ring for a taxi and he would come and collect her and whisk her away from there at breakneck speed. She smiled at his kind face and tried to give him a tip, which he wouldn't accept. When he'd gone, she stood alone in the fading smell of the exhaust fumes and listened. A pair of hunting owls hooted to one another somewhere quite close. She thought she could hear a television or a radio. A shard of yellow light lay like an arrow across the snow from a gap in a curtain. She had been deposited at what seemed like a back door, judging from the shapes of coats and Wellingtons she could see through its panes. She knocked on the glass and heard the scrape of a chair being pushed back. The light was switched on and Leo Spring was there opening the door, smiling his smile and ushering her in. He must have been waiting for her alone in this huge and dimly lit kitchen. She glanced at the open copy of *Bleak House*, the half-empty bottle of wine, the remains of some bread and cheese, as he took her coat and gently led her towards a ladder-backed chair.

He hardly mentioned the garden that evening.

He offered her a glass of wine, which she hesitantly accepted, feeling its bitter sweetness in her throat, softening her fear. He told her about his family, about how his father and mother had kept an open house here in the seventies, about how he had travelled the world and now would stay here for ever. She told him some elaborate lies about her time at horticultural college.

It transpired that she would not be staying in the house at all. He led the way back out into the courtyard and along a slippery path by torchlight to the stable block. She followed, lugging her suitcase and her plastic bag of books. He switched on the light to reveal a large open-plan space with coconut mats and a ladder up to a loft where she imagined the bed was. In the centre of the room a noisy, old-fashioned fan heater had been left to blow. There was an enormous faded leather chaise longue in the centre of the room, a bright rug with geometric patterns on it and some strange seventies-looking macramé decorations.

He saw her looking, wondering. 'Parents had it converted way back, but it's never been used much. There's a kitchen area in that corner and a bathroom behind that partition.'

It seemed strange that he should have decided to put her here when there was a whole house. She looked at his large, preoccupied face.

'Thought you'd prefer this somehow,' he said. 'House is all shut up anyway. I end up sort of camping in one bit.'

He was right, of course. And she was only the

gardener, after all. Her eyes wandered to the desk. They wished each other good-night and she watched the torch beam float back to the house.

What a strange thing I have done, she thought. Can he possibly believe that I am what I say I am? Does he care? She thought of his strange and beautiful face, like a Botticelli angel, his faded-looking eyes, the soft ringlets of his pale brown hair. It is not really the garden which occupies his thoughts, she surmised; it is something, or someone, else. And then she climbed up the ladder to the loft part, where she found a high, iron-framed bed with an Indian quilt on it and a hot water bottle inside it.

'I could never have imagined this,' she said aloud as she opened her journal and christened its first, gleaming white page.

9

LEO

In the morning it was raining and the snow had disappeared. Leo was managing to shave and look out of the window at the same time, having elongated the zigzags of his chrome shaving-mirror to their fullest extent. He could see the rain coming in across the fields. He looked down to the courtyard below and saw the gardener girl standing in the stable doorway. From this distance she looked more like a gardener boy. Valentina did not seem the right name for her.

There were pigeons sitting soddenly in the eaves, dark bluey grey against the red, shining tiles. They looked long-suffering and he felt sorry for them and wondered how it was that when he was a boy he had tried to kill them with his air rifle. He knew the courtyard gateposts were dotted with indentations where his shots had gone astray. His childhood was a place he wanted to go back to. He wanted Beech House to be like it was when he was a boy. The garden had been beginning to go even then, but that was twenty years ago. He thought of Melody. He saw her in a soft, straw hat weighed down with roses and two long pink ribbons hanging down on either side. She was wearing a floaty dress, made of something he thought of as being gossamer, although he did not really know what this was. Her feet were bare, faintly brown against the grass. He seemed to look upwards at her body from ground level. And then he realised it was his mother he saw and not Melody at all. He was remembering a summer's day, a summer garden party long ago. He seemed to hear music coming from the house and yet he could not decipher what it was. He longed to hear that music again but found he could not quite remember it, or hear it in his mind, however hard he tried. When he looked back at the stable door, it was closed.

10
VALENTINA

Valentina was sitting dressed at the desk under the window, looking at the sheep grazing miserably in the wet. She was leafing through the pages of a photograph album that Leo had left with some old gardening books he must have found in the house. She presumed it was so she could see in the backgrounds of the photographs what the garden was like in its heyday. She saw only him, like a white piece of cloud, drifting through the pictures of his childhood, sitting on the edges of picnics, playing with an enormous dog. She recognised his wide eyes, his ringlety hair. The knock at the door didn't startle her. It was a light knock. Unassuming. She let the album thud softly shut. She put on her giant waterproof and went to receive her employer. They walked out of the stable yard towards the foggy grasslands, Leo batting at the undergrowth with a long, cleft stick. Valentina felt herself being drawn to his side.

11

MELODY

The day was damp and grey. The snowdrops grew out of a sea of mud beneath the cherry tree in the front garden. The first catkins, which had gyrated in the wind yesterday, today hung limply across her window, a lurid yellow against the darkening sky. It was Valentine's Day. Melody was sitting by the electric fire trying to find the will to go for a walk because she knew that it would cheer her up but not feeling cheerful enough to rise from the chair. A bunch of snowdrops lay in her lap from an earlier foray out into the sodden garden. She thought they were like little corpses. There were two cards on the mantelpiece: an enormous heart that looked as though it had been printed in blood and which contained the black words *Be Mine* in Leo Spring's unmistakably flamboyant handwriting, and another one. The other card was a mystery. It was small and delicate and covered in flirtatious pink tissue-paper roses, which could only have been home made. Its unrecognisable handwriting was baby blue and told her it loved her. Unmoved by its sentiments and completely unable to think who it could possibly be from, she wrenched herself up, took the snow-drops to the sink and plonked them in a convenient jam jar.

The river was up over the bottom of the garden, brown, gushing and unstoppable and bearing debris, which would be left strewn on the lawn when it subsided. She listened to the rain starting to drum once more on the slates. She saw a gang of her pupils walking over the bridge with their hoods up. One of the boys, Fitch, looked up to the window and saw her. She gave a little wave. He waved back, his embarrassed face half obscured by his hood. She thought about school. She had told Mr Boase in January that she would not be coming back for the foreseeable future. She thought, no future is seeable. She went to hunt for her umbrella and Gabriel's waterproof coat that still smelt of him and had pockets full of flakes of his tobacco. She slammed the door behind her and strode down the street in the opposite direction to the children. She thought, I will go to the castle and look out from the ramparts and force myself to embrace my future that I cannot see. And as she walked along, and the blood began to pump heat into her body, she had the strange sensation of Gabriel's coat being an arm around her, protecting her, and this gave her the courage to go on with her walk and not to think that all was lost and that she would never fall in love and would be alone for the rest of her life. After all, she had received two valentines and one of them was a genuine mystery, although it was probably not beyond Leo to have sent both. As she walked across the green in the middle of Illerwick, she saw that, despite the rain, the trees were full of chattering starlings and it was a curiously uplifting sound.

12
LEO

Leo went to Kew. He was looking for something, but he wasn't quite sure what it was. It could have been inspiration. Or it could have been something else, something more specific. He had travelled to London by car, distanced from the weather by a warm cocoon of black leather upholstery, and so it seemed to him that the garden was another country with its own climate, a climate of ferocious winds. Everything was empty. Although this was called the Main Gate, this was not the gate he remembered entering the gardens by in the past. He hesitated on the broad path, his hair whipping around his face, blinding him and filling him with irritation. He battened it down with his scarf and as he forged ahead, parallel to the river, past all the blown-over benches, he thought, I am like an Arabian nomad struggling along in the desert winds of the Sahara.

Dimly, he remembered a view of Syon House on the other side of the river. He knew of someone who had held their wedding reception there, their wedding breakfast. The idea of a wedding breakfast seemed enchanting to him. He thought of

Melody; a throng of people, the ghosts of his past, were the guests. And he saw it at last, farther away than he had thought, like a house painted onto the backdrop of a stage in muted colours. Was this why he had come? The lion on the ramparts reminded him of himself and his own inadequacies and his mane tied down. He veered off through the trees in the direction that the wind seemed to blow him. The leaves of eucalyptus, oak and pine roared at him behind his back. He hurried on until the Temperate House began to appear. He felt a flutter of excitement as though he had nearly arrived at the thing he was looking for. He glanced to his left towards smaller trees and grass and had a vague recollection of being young and lying there with a girl one summer's day. Who was this girl? He could not remember. Was this why he had come? To be reminded of the passing of his youth? To have an early flowering cherry scatter a confetti of petals over him in some kind of mockery?

The Temperate House was arranged in countries but he did not realise this at first. He was just aware of a change in atmosphere, of a feeling of warmth and the smell of soil. As he climbed the spiral staircase, he looked down at the pond full of carp with arum lilies round it. Was it the smell of the lilies that was so heavy in the air? He breathed it in and felt a familiar longing for love wash over him. He was intoxicated by scents and his eyes were dazzled in a moment of vertigo by the innumerable geometric shapes of glass and the fronds and fans of palms and long, long shoots like arms stretching up into the emptiness of the warm air. Then a terrible roaring started up.

At first it sounded like a crowd of boys let loose, but it went on too long for that. He thought of a madman, of someone in the throes of a terrible fit. The old couples, the American women in nice anoraks putting on glasses to read the plant labels and the children on half-term outings, all paused, listening, animal-like amongst the leaves. He made his way towards Australia and saw that it was cordoned off. Some men in traditional South Sea Island dress were being filmed against the palm fronds making war cries and stamping their feet. Their hair was tied up in topknots and they had dark patterns painted on their faces. A man was holding lights above them and someone was calling instructions from a platform hidden in the leaves. Leo imagined a close-up in an adventure film, terrifying faces zoomed-in, the illusion of a rainforest that stretched for hundreds of miles behind them. In between takes, someone made a joke and the South Sea Island men's laughter was high and girlish in the greenness. He thought, life is full of illusions.

Outside, the furry buds of the magnolia were almost bursting open. The sky was gunmetal grey but, from somewhere, bright light came and fidgeted in the blowing surface of the lake, catching in the beginnings of tiny bright green buds and illuminating the petals of the jonquils. Was that their name? He would ask Valentina. He wandered sadly down the path that cut through the 'crocus carpet'. This was where all the people were, crowding in through the Victoria Gate and milling about near the gift shop and the cafeteria. A sign told him that, in the wild, the carpet of crocus flowers comes when the snow melts in the mountains of the Pyrenees. He wanted to be in the mountains now and to be breathing the clear mountain air instead of the London air that was tinged with pollution even here, and to discover a crocus carpet that was a genuine surprise, a gift. He could not deny the beauty of these white and purple flowers stretching into the distance on the muddy grass. They were not in their right home, perhaps, like the Turkish carpets at Beech House that didn't really belong on the Welsh oak boards. But then, he reflected, that is part of the pleasure, the bringing of exoticism from all over the world. Nearly everything in this garden was transported from somewhere else in the world, once.

It was like a steam bath in the Palm House. He wandered among the pepper plants, the African nutmeg orchid, the papaya and mango, the banana leaves like rolled cigars, the ebony tree. Then he saw it. The coco de mer. And he knew, all at once, that this was what he had searched for, without knowing it. This is it, he thought. I will have my very own Palm House built in my own grounds and Melody will walk there with me in the steam. We will be like Adam and Eve in Paradise. A laugh escaped him that sounded like a sob. A woman sitting on a bench reading her newspaper eyed him, pausing momentarily in the chewing of a mouthful of crusty bread. The voices of children echoed high, high above like birds on the wrought iron balustrades.

When he emerged, it was starting to rain and he became caught up in a troop of American tourists making their way to their Explorer Bus, which promised them a tour of Kew in forty minutes. A girdle round the earth. I will do it, he thought. He swerved away from them, feeling his coat tails flapping, his ringlets tightening in the rain and dreaming of Melody's bottom, which he knew would be as perfect as the coco de mer.

13

FITCH

Fitch was sitting on his bedroom floor. Then he was standing by the window. Then he was lying on his bed, staring at the familiar map of striations and woodworm holes on the beams onto which he plotted his daily thoughts. Down below he heard his father stumping in from the garden; voices on the radio; potatoes thudding into the stainless steel sink. Outside: birdsong, lambs, a farm vehicle, the faint cries of a football match he didn't care about. He picked up a piece of driftwood he had been carving and turned it over and over in the light. It was becoming a face, a woman's face. Whose was it? It changed from day to day.

Day after day he watched his father talking to himself in the vegetable patch from his high port-hole window. His father was keeping himself busy binding things, twining, tying things down with his thick, red fingers. He withstood all weathers. When he sat on the rusty old roller the dogs sat at his feet and rested their white muzzles on his knees gently. They fixed their eyes on him but he didn't meet their gaze. He fished out his glasses and studied the backs of seed packets or unfolded the *Echo* and read it in sections.

Sometimes there was the rattle of the van as he disappeared on undisclosed missions down the lane. Fitch never questioned him about where he had been. His father never questioned Fitch. He knew what it was to be a boy round here. He knew what it was to be a boy in this house. He had lain on this very bed dreaming his own dreams, plotting his own thoughts. His sweethearts were now the mothers of the girls in Fitch's class. Suzy's mother had been his sweetheart. Sweetheart was his word.

His father's father had been a gypsy but that way of life came to an end. This is where they had laid down their roots. They had never strayed since. They got by. His mother was the only one who couldn't stick it here. She unravelled her ties quick enough. His father had tried to keep her for too long. He admitted that. She had brown eyes which absorbed things deeply. She had tiny hands that fluttered when she talked. These were the two things his father had told him he had loved. The eyes and the hands. Lying on the white candlewick bedspread, a vestige of her, Fitch tried to fall through time until he could sense her somewhere near him. He studied the photograph they had of her leaning in the doorway of the cottage. She was looking beyond the hedge and over the sea to America. Her crossed arms were dusky. She had a plait of hair. Her blouse billowed out over her breasts as though in a gust of wind. Inside the blouse was her heart which longed for things that could not be found in Illerwick. Things which no one there could provide.

His father kept his longing for her contained in the vegetable patch. He was rooted there, his clothes faded like broccoli leaves. Some evenings, though, he would be drawn through the dew of the evening to Fitch doing his homework at the kitchen table. To Fitch, staring at incomprehensible combinations of numbers. He thought they were gobbledegook but he did not tell his father this. He tried to make sense of them. He inadvertently wrote them back to front and created disasters, explosions of numbers which caused Mr Boase to fly into rages the next day. He juggled notes inside his head in the spaces where numbers would have slotted in neatly if he had let them. He allowed his mind to drift towards the soft notes of his father's tin whistle which he played in the evenings. They ate their tea in silence often as not. Often it was wet and dripping outside. Planes crossed over them, out of sight.

14

MR BOASE

Mr Boase sat for a long time at Miss Vye's desk. The pupils preferred her room and were therefore marginally better behaved in it. Since he had been in sole charge of her teaching, he had stipulated that all lessons would be held there. And he had his own secret reasons for occupying it. Now there was a dusting of chalk over everything, which had never been there before. He regretted this, but it couldn't be helped. It had accumulated during the stale afternoons of recent weeks as he had crushed chalk after chalk in his effort to explain algebraic equations. The sleeves of his navy blazer had turned grey with it. He touched his few tufts of hair where the dust had mingled with Brylcreem into a kind of stickiness. He felt old. He thought about the valentine he had sent her. It gave him a somersaulting feeling he was not used to; it had been both frivolous and daring.

It was difficult to run the school without her. The children were taking advantage of her absence to play merry hell. He thought of the boy, Fitch, whose obtuseness had caused him to throw the board rubber that afternoon and how the boy had caught it, in surprise, and thrown it back. He heard the laughter dance through the room again. He picked up the board rubber and hurled it out at the space where their goading faces had been. It bounced off the back wall and skittered across the floor. It was time to go home. The cleaners had already left. He slid open the drawer of Miss Vye's desk and rifled through its contents. He flicked through her neatly filled in register. He traced the delicate handwriting on the label of her mark book with his little finger. He licked the spine of her diary with the tip of his tongue. In the back of the drawer he saw a screwed up handkerchief. Hers. Trembling, he unscrunched it and held it over his face, smelling. He let it rest there, sucking it with wet lips. His nostrils blew it in and out in little puffs. He imagined her covering him, her hair falling over him, her soft breasts against his mouth. The somersaulting feeling was there again, then a tightness in his groin. He found himself panting, longing for her. He undid his trousers and clutched with his chalky fingers. He pressed himself against the front of the drawer. He heard himself groaning, then stillness and the ticking of the classroom clock.

A movement. A rustle. A wind rippling through the room. He opened his eyes to a shadow, something, a darkness crossing the room. Something was there in the corner. He went towards it, to the space between the atlas cupboard and the wall. He saw a boy cowering there. Fitch. Vomit rose in his throat in horror of what he must have seen. He opened and closed his mouth. There were no words for this. Only his body shaking.

'I forgot my textbook, Sir. It's for the homework tonight, Mr Boase. Please don't hit me. The door was open, Sir. I thought you were in your office.'

He lunged for the boy. He had no thoughts, only feelings that he could not control.

Suddenly the boy was ramming a desk into him, shunting him aside, leaping over the ranks of chairs. He swivelled round to see him, breathless in the doorway, his face red, his black hair standing on end. Their eyes met.

'Wanker!' he shrieked. 'Wanker!' he screamed as his footsteps squeaked down the corridor.

Boase let himself sink to the floor. He pressed his cheek against the cool tiles. The dust was even here, somersaulting in a shaft of the dying light. Dust to dust, he thought.

Fitch was still running. Running down Broad Street, round Dog Lane, past the post office, out into the fields, past the tyre mountain by the Evans's farm. In the distance, against the darkening woods, he could still see the outline of the castle. He kept running, on and on.

Boase got up from the floor. He picked up the desk. He spent a long time straightening the chairs in line with the tiles. He picked up the handkerchief and put it in his pocket and straightened his bow tie. He blew the dust off his books and dropped them one by one into his briefcase. He snapped it shut. He closed one of the high windows with a long wooden pole. It was nearly dark when he emerged into the playground and he stood for a moment and stared at the black lace of the trees, debating. He went to The Crown. He walked towards its golden windows. He looked inside where he could see the landlord, Jack Flagg, and all his cronies gathered round the bar. There was a fire. He stood there for a long time looking, trying to catch the drift of the conversation and failing, looking at the redness of it all. Then he pressed onwards to the Brydges Gate Estate where he lived alone in modern, mathematical tidiness. As he walked, he shuffled through his mind images of his student days like cards: the spew, the unsuccessful fumbles with girls, the jumping off Magdalen Bridge on a May morning. And later, drinking alone in his flat in Kilburn, the quick nips before work, the sickness of self-loathing. Through the window of the Londis shop, he saw the bottles of whisky gleaming in jolly rows.

Fitch was standing on the ramparts in the dark. He was not afraid. He listened to the swirling of the wind in the trees and knew he would not go back to school. He thought about running away. He thought of his father. He walked home slowly via the grounds of Leo Spring's house and saw that the stable was occupied by a young man with his back to the window cleaning the blades of a pair of shears. He went home to where his father was waiting for him holding a frying pan. The dark eyes reproached him for a second, then melted. They ate bacon and eggs and watched *The Good, the Bad and the Ugly* on TV. In the morning, Fitch lay on his back and heard the school bus creak past. It stopped for a moment and then rumbled on. He went to his book-shelf and pulled out a book he had loved when he was ten called *Natural Wonders of the World*.

He turned the pages with exaggerated care until his father came and said, 'Not well, my boy?'

'No.'

He came in and felt Fitch's forehead. They looked at one another for a long time. Then his father went away. Fitch saw him, later, sitting on the roller stroking the dogs. He got himself a cheese sand-wich for lunch.

In the evening he said to his father, 'Something happened at school. I can't go there any more. If you make me I will have to run away.'

His father hesitated and Fitch knew he should not have said this because whatever happened they would never abandon one another. Then his father said, 'Well, if that's how you feel, that's how you feel.'

The next day Boase went to the pub and ordered a pint of bitter. It slid down with perfect ease. The taste, even after twenty-five years, was familiar and comforting. He left it at that. He felt normal. He congratulated himself on being able to leave it at that. Nothing untoward happened as a result of drinking the beer. It softened the events of the night before. The boy, he had noticed, had not come to school. He began to think that Fitch had no power. He began to think that it would never be alluded to.

15

VALENTINA

Valentina was in the kitchen garden. She liked the warmth of its orange walls and its feeling of enclosure. She walked along the brick paths matted with moss and self-seeded forget-me-nots. There were fruit trees, pears or plums, just coming into flower on the south-facing wall. On that first tour with Leo, she had counted twelve lichen-coated apple trees in minuscule leaf and bud and in each one a knot of mistletoe. The vegetable garden was a sea of ground elder and dried-up Michaelmas daisies. Someone had put down sheets of tarpaulin and rotting old carpets to damp down the weeds. In the grass, celandines glinted.

She kicked away the heaps of dried-up leaves in front of the greenhouse doors and went in. It was about three times the size of an ordinary greenhouse. The panes were green with moss and algae and some of them were cracked or broken. She breathed in the dry smell of terracotta pots and ancient tomato plants. Through the end windows she could see the remnants of the herb garden. There were dry stalks of mint with dark sage leaves growing in between them as far as some caved-in fruit cages. On the left of these were a few rose bushes, which must have been for flower arrangements. She went back outside into the delicate veil of blackbird-singing. A cabbage white butterfly flew past her like a ghost.

On the other side of the house were the terraced herbaceous borders edged by towering, unclipped box and yew hedges and the lawns. Using the books she had brought with her, she had begun to make notes of what it was possible to salvage and what it would be necessary to cut back severely. Leo had mentioned topiary animals for the yew. She found him sitting glumly in the orangery, looking out from beneath a swathe of Russian vine across the lawns towards the woods. He hadn't seen her and she stood for a moment watching him, following his gaze that seemed to be looking far beyond the garden, and her heartbeats quickened. He heard the gravel shifting beneath her feet and called out to her, nodding approvingly at her notebook.

'How did it get into this state?' she said, when she was sitting beside him on one of the wrought iron benches inside, but she was smiling because she could sense his guilt at letting things go.

'Being abroad? The research for my instrument book took eight years. No doubt I outstayed my welcome in various far-flung corners of the globe. I know I've been away too long.'

'Imagine all this when it was at its peak.'

'It was my mother who kept it going – she had a green-fingered phase in her latter years – and then when she died it just sort of existed by itself for a while and it's gone wild by degrees. I think Patrick, the last gardener, died while I was away.'

'I'll need help,' Valentina said. 'I know what you've said about money and there is the upkeep of the house to think of but it'll take more than just me if you really want to tackle this, however strong I am.' She knew that this made the project sound important, like a plan of campaign. She thought desperately of the need to enlist the help of someone who really knew about plants. A bona fide gardener.

Leo looked disappointed. He stared sadly at the cypress trees. The murmur of pigeons filled the silence between them as the enormity of their task and the amount of physical labour involved sank in. Valentina sensed there was something else in Leo's mind, besides the garden.

'I'll advertise,' he said, at last. 'I do realise that you're the designer in all this, not the hard labour. How many extra gardeners can we run to? One? Two? You'll have to help me with the finances.'

She smiled at him but didn't answer his question. She needed time to think. She said, 'I must get on with clearing the leaves from the fountain. The plumber is coming this afternoon.' And she went down the path towards an empty wheelbarrow she had discovered earlier in one of the outhouses.

When she looked back later he was still there, sitting like a sad statue, the weight of greenery all about him. What he needs, she thought, are some jobs of his own to do, and she started to think of a few practical tasks that would not be beyond him, such as cleaning the greenhouse windows. In the afternoon, the boy came for his piano lesson. He waved.

'Would you like a Saturday job?' she asked him when he was within earshot.

'Depends how much I'd get paid,' he said, staring at her strangely, as though he half recognised her.

'I'll get back to you,' she said.

16
MELODY

The end of August. That last summer. Melody is lying in the hammock under the biggest beech tree of the lawns. She can feel the string of the hammock cutting diamonds into her thighs like mermaid scales. She runs her fingertips tentatively across the cushions of flesh underneath her rucked-up summery dress and thinks about her future trans-formation when she has left Illerwick. She is lolling with her head tilted back so that when she opens her right eye, she can see a skewed version of Beech House, its tall barley-sugar chimneys imprinted on a royal blue sky. If she lets her head roll over, with her other eye, in the tree's vast tent of shade, she can see Leo and Gabriel lying on their stomachs on either side of a large chessboard. They are unaware of her, distanced in their other world, caught up in the mirrored movements of their game. For days they have been ensconced in curtained rooms watching chess on TV, learning new moves. They are just out of earshot, on the border of the deep shadow, as though at the sea's edge. They dip their long bare feet into the bright heat of the lawn and then withdraw them when they feel them burn. Butterflies settle on their toes but they do not seem to notice them. Snatches of their voices and low laughter reach her then are lost. They are learning to smoke.

She closes her eyes and listens to the susurration of the leaves, to her own breathing: waves of sound getting bigger and smaller. Later, they will play tennis, the ball thudding flatly on the small-headed rackets they found in the summerhouse, which Gabriel says are made of cats' guts. On the tennis court, she will come into her own. She will have changed into her tennis dress and in her mind she will be transformed into a different girl, her hair smooth and blonde, her skin the colour of butter-scotch. It will just be her and Gabriel, pitted against each other. Leo will watch and act as umpire, chanting the score in his Wimbledon voice. She will feel Leo's eyes upon her as the substitute eyes of future boyfriends. She will feel her body move where she wants it to. It will be like dancing. While they are playing, the evening will fall around them, the flowers will whiten in the dusk, releasing musky scents and the grass will dampen.

They will retreat to the stable and Gabriel will produce a bottle which he will have pilfered from the house. Leo will smile lazily, badly rolling an enormous joint in the manner of his heroes at school. He is working his way through his parents' record collection. Tonight it will be Jimi Hendrix. 'Purple Haze'. They will venture out into the velvet darkness, whirl around the dark lawns, trail their hands in the fountain. They will bump into each other. Leo will kiss her lightly, she will kiss Gabriel, Gabriel will kiss Leo. It won't mean anything. In the morning, the other two will still be asleep, end to end on the enormous chaise longue, unaware of their touching feet, like lovers, like the butterflies, oblivious to the sound of a lawn-mower, to the cries of peacocks. Her thoughts will drift slowly back to real life and to her self-improvement programme. To how many miles she must cycle, how many calories she can allow herself, how many centimetres of flesh she must lose in order to achieve her transformation. But she will know it is nearly too late.

That day they will go to the beach. They will lie on the uncomfortable, hot stones in the angle of cliff where they have always lain, swim in the gloopy, seaweedy water, shiver. She will try to exist for once in the now, smiling too much at the others to try to melt the hard pebble in her throat, rubbing frantically at the tar stains on her hands because this is the last day of the summer and tomorrow she is going to Cambridge.

17
VALENTINA

The weather changed. Valentina and Leo sat opposite each other in the high, red armchairs. Leo was putting record after record on the gramophone. Sometimes he would keep playing the same record, saying he wanted to hear a particular phrase again and again. He assumed she recognised each piece. She felt saturated by the notes, as if the storm going on beyond the brocade curtains was happening all inside the room. From far away, she heard the monsoons of her childhood.

It was hot in the room, so hot the whole of her right side itched, but she did not dare to, or want to, move. She looked at him now, his head on one side, cigarette smoke streaming from his nostrils. He seemed to thrive in the heat, like a salamander. He had invited her in to discuss plans for the garden and she had come shyly and awkwardly into his red room; now the plans lay strewn around, like discarded clothes. He had told her about an idea he had conceived at Kew to construct a palm house. He had leapt around the room, making dome and arch shapes with his arms.

The fire crackled. A larch tree brushed the windows. They sat motionless, contemplating, drinking red wine. Valentina breathed in the spicy smell of the wine, the smoke from Leo's cigarettes, the different smoke of the fire and the smell of books and dust and aged upholstery. He turned to her. She knew he was going to speak but suddenly she didn't want him to. She saw his lips begin to form her name. And then she knew it would be a confession. The confession of a thing that she could not bear to hear. It was too soon. She half got up from her seat and sat down again. Leo did not notice.

'Valentina?' Valentina did not reply. She could not stop him now. 'Valentina. You know the garden project is not just for me. It is for someone in partic- ular who I see living and breathing in it. Gracing it, after all the hard work is done.' The windows trembled in the wind.

'Anyone I know?' she said nonchalantly. She knew no one except Fitch.

Leo seemed not to hear her. He went on, 'It's madness, really and I know it and yet it is all for her. My life is for her. I am, indeed, lost.'

He smiled raffishly, but with his mouth only, leaving his eyes stranded. Somewhere there was a pride in all this silly sadness. Valentina looked at him steadfastly and thought, I am doomed. The burning root shifted on the fire.

'Her name is Melody.'

He said this with a kind of delight as though her name explained everything.

'Melody *Vye*,' he said impressively. 'I want to marry her.'

Valentina arranged her face into a smile. She knew who it was now. She was the headmistress. Fitch had said, 'The piano lessons were all Miss Vye's idea,' as though he meant fault.

It seemed as though the conversation would stop there. But it did not. Leo put on a Chopin nocturne. He said that Melody Vye had always lived in Illerwick but that, at first, he had not noticed her. He had been away at boarding-school and then one summer he had come back for the holidays and there she was. She was the vicar's daughter and he had first seen her in church. She had been sitting in front of him, so close that he could have reached out and unfurled one of the tiny tendrils of hair at the nape of her neck. She had been sitting very straight and very still throughout her father's sermon and the light through the stained glass window had made outlandish psychedelic patterns on her cheek.

'But it was her brother who became my friend,' he said at last. He turned away, his long hands shielding his eyes. 'He has killed himself. She won't see me.'

Valentina got up to go. She had been wrong. Everything was wrong now. It was wrong, now, to be here in this hot room in the middle of this but he leaned forward in his chair and stopped her.

'Wait. Listen. I want you to go and see her. Introduce yourself. Think of some reason why you have to see her. I want you to see how beautiful she is so you understand. She won't see me. I want you to tell her.'

'Tell her what?' Why did she have to understand? Why had she made herself so ugly?

'Be my go-between, Valentina. It's my last hope,' he said.

'Excuse me,' she said politely and removed herself.

Outside the world was roaring and wild. She ran through the darkness clutching at her spikes of hair.

18

MELODY

Four months ago. New Year's Eve. Leo is driving. They are returning from the restaurant of The Three Feathers Hotel. Not returning home, but returning to the sea, driving to Breakers Point as though it is a magnet pulling them. The car slices through the cold air, speeding through iced darkness. Melody's stomach is a tight knot. The dinner was awkward, the hotel raucous, hot and merry. He'd tried to tell her about the musical instruments of Borneo. His gestures, his flailing arms had embarrassed her. His hair had embarrassed her. She had watched as he had run his fingers through it, transferring butter and crumbs from his side plate into its coils. The hedgerows are mad, black scribbles in the headlights, tall and enclosing on the tops of high banks. They are in a tunnel not of love but of despair. Only she can see this. Eyes glow suddenly in the stiffened grasses and then are gone. The green digital numbers embedded in the dashboard say 11:47.

She can hear a bottle of champagne rolling wildly on the back seat, clinking against the seatbelt clasps.

Leo's voice is rippling on about places far away which only he can see in his mind's eye. He is making the blowing sounds of pipes, drumming the skin of the steering wheel. She tries to listen to other sounds: to the tyres swishing on wet tarmac, to the wind buffeting the window. The landscape is hidden, deathly. She wants to go home. She should never have left Gabriel on his own. Leo's hand brushes her leg as he changes gear. A spray of rain scatters over the windscreen like small stones.

They roll into the deserted car park on the edge of the cliffs. Leo is pleased that it is deserted. He laughs to think that there is no one else here. He fumbles in the back for the bottle, pressing against her side, pushing on her thigh. Her stomach has closed down. The thought of more alcohol in it makes her want to be sick. She gets out and the wind is like a slap. They stand side by side and look across the strait. The tiny lights on the farther shore are apertures in a dark wall to somewhere more exciting. The sea is rasping below them, a terrible heavy breathing in the dark. Premature fireworks are pink and green damp squibs. There is no moon.

Leo says, 'I think we'd better do this inside.' He holds up the bottle. The glass stems are twisted between his long, pianist's fingers. A smile: hopeful, yet sad.

They get back in the car. Now it's cold there too. The green numbers say 11:58. He turns the key in the ignition. For a second she thinks that he is going to drive off the cliff but then there is the whirr of the heating coming on. 12:00. She looks away as he struggles with the cork, the glasses, watching her stupid reflection. The cork bangs on the car roof and then he is pushing a brimming glass towards her. His eyes are bright and glistening in the yellowy light. She feels his hot breath against her face, his hair tickling. He does not put anything into words but presses a small velvet box, like a cat's paw, into her palm, his lips, his open mouth falling onto hers. She feels the wetness of his tongue, then struggles from him. Out of the car, she gulps the cold air, stumbling over the tussocky grass. He stays inside, a black heap of coat.

They drive back to Illerwick in silence, past the black hedges and the dead landscape. Illerwick's New Year's Eve is going on behind closed curtains. A few strangers are getting into cars in the car park of The Crown in a dumb show of hilarity. Leo parks outside her house and blurts out some things that he had planned to say earlier but now there are tears and snot spurting from his face. He takes her hand in his wet fingers. She drags it free and slams the door.

Gabriel is waiting by the fire in darkness. She turns on the light. When he sees her face he seems to smile slightly but he is trembling.

19
LEO

Valentina trudged past the library window dragging a large sack, interrupting Leo's view of the tennis court where there had been a mirage of a teenage Melody dancing about in her immaculate tennis whites. Valentina, who now, admittedly, was doing the hard labour, looked dirty and unkempt. With her short-back-and-sides and make-up-less face she reminded him more than anything of a boy. But he liked having a female gardener; it was unconventional.

Sitting in the library with the window open, he heard the curlews' mating calls as they flew over the garden on their way to the river and he knew he was entering yet another loveless spring. In the past, in his university days, he had scores of girl-friends and he had thought himself in love often, but then he would see Melody again, their paths would cross and the girlfriends would fade away. He unfolded the January letter from Melody and darkness clouded the garden scheme in his mind for a while. In a wave, he felt the loss of Gabriel, his only friend, who would listen and understand.

That afternoon he went down to the bottom of the kitchen garden and continued cleaning the greenhouse windows. Despite himself, he had found that it was a rewarding job. Valentina was there in the periphery of his vision, emerging occasionally from the middle of a flowerbed with leaves sticking to her. After a while, she seemed like part of the garden, nothing more than a pigeon or a black-bird. He liked having people in the background, though. He liked the plan of teaching Fitch – he had Melody to thank for that. He longed for her presence and yet here he was with only Fitch and Valentina as companions, Fitch more than ever now that he was doing the Saturday job. He stopped and watched them moving to and fro, like twins, with armfuls of weeds to the barrow. For an instant, Valentina was framed in a pane of glass, and as his wiping made the glass clearer, a thought came in a rush, like a crossword clue, which made him smile. It was an explanation of her.

Fitch was due to stop work in half an hour to come for his lesson so Leo meandered inside, stop-ping to smell the viburnum and to admire the magnolia, now in full flower. He plucked a magnolia petal and crushed it between his fingers as he walked up to the house, still smiling to himself in a Sherlock Holmes kind of way. Fitch had been learning *Für Elise* but it was obvious he hadn't been practising. Leo was no good at lecturing people so he just said nothing and cut the lesson short. He led Fitch up to a room on the second floor where he kept the instruments he had collected. He took them out one by one and got Fitch to guess how they were played. After a while, Leo asked why Fitch had not been practising. Fitch didn't answer. Leo knew it would be to do with the school. Perhaps that tedious old fool, Boase, had something to do with it. After all, Melody wasn't around to keep order there now. He knew they didn't have a piano at home. He thought, benevolently, of getting the piano in the old nursery transported to their cottage but then he thought this would perhaps be taken wrongly. There probably wasn't room anyway.

In the end he said, lightly, 'You can come and practise up here at weekends if you like. No one uses the piano in the nursery. You'd be up here anyway doing your Saturday job and I certainly wouldn't disturb you.'

Fitch seemed embarrassed by the idea so he didn't press him. The word nursery had probably not helped.

20
MELODY

Gabriel is watching her from the top of the cliff. She's supposed to be watching him. He's burning things with the lenses of the bird-watching binoculars they borrowed from Daddy. He seems so high up there on the edge of the blue sky. She feels self-consciously aware of his guarding eyes, zooming her in and out, boring into her and then turning her into a speck. Then she goes further and further among the rocks and rock pools and forgets him. She steps, like a giant, from peak to peak above lakes of red blobs and scuttling things. She moves farther away from the familiar line of rotting seaweed until she can feel strong, salty gusts against her face. The bladderwrack floats like monstrous hair as the sea breathes in and out.

21
FITCH

Fitch was walking through the coolness of the beech woods in the shade, past splodges of bluebells, underneath green, silky leaves, which had just unfurled. Then along main roads, dusty with traffic, past scrubby verges of lengthening grass and the beginnings of cow parsley. Then he was cutting across fields to a dirty bit of beach where Pete and the others came to hide and secretly smoke and read back copies of *Penthouse* they got from Dave. He could do that if he wanted. He did do that sometimes. His private imaginings, when she was Melody, he kept in another section of his mind. He kicked things about for a while and prodded at the cold remains of someone's fire with a stick and then moved on. He let the sea rumble on in the background.

He had left early, before there was any warmth in the sun. Illerwick had been shrouded in an eerie mist, the hills invisible. Then the sun was solid on his back pushing him forward, like a guiding hand. There is no need to keep doing this, he thought. But then Boase came suddenly into his mind. The lost expression on his face. The sound that came out of him. The way he changed personality when she was near, his small eyes widening behind his glasses, the hint of a smile creeping to the corners of his lips. Fitch thought of his elbow-patched arm draped around Miss Vye when he told her about her brother. She could never see it. Or if she did, she ignored it. She had already had a lifetime of men drooling over her. It was the curse of being beautiful.

He hung around the next place, Porth Gwyn, for a bit. He sat in a lonely bus shelter and carved his name in the creosoted wood with a piece of glass. He did not carve hers. Suzy would have drawn a heart with an arrow through it next to her name. His name would probably be stuck on the end of it. He did not draw a heart, or even a question mark. He just left a significant space. A bus didn't come so he wandered up and down the pedestrian precinct, which was already starting to get busy with depressed-looking people buying things from Woolworth's and hovering over cheap shoes. He bought a pie from a bakery and then threw it away after one mouthful. Some kids, fellow truants, eyed him and then decided to give him the cold shoulder. He ended up in a graveyard. Someone was having an early morning funeral. He watched the proceedings from behind a statue. He noticed, among the mourners, a boy about his own age with a bleached, uncrying face. There was a time when he had thought his own mother was dead. He used to imagine her funeral in the hot dry earth of what his father called the U S of A, sand blowing, getting into the eyes of the solitary preacher who buried her and no one and nothing in sight, except tumble-weed rolling by like in the movies.

But she hadn't died at all. She hadn't even gone to America. All the things he had thought had been assumptions that he had painted on to the canvas of his father's silence. They had visited her a few years ago. They'd gone up to London on the train, his father stiff in a shirt and trousers he didn't normally wear. He had refused to wear the smart clothes his father had laid out for him because he had wanted her to see what he wore in real life. He'd imagined her eyes when she saw him being full of pride but everything about that day that he had imagined had turned out differently. The flat was near the top of a tower block and the lift had been broken so they had had to go up hundreds of concrete stairs that looked as though they would crack your head open if you slipped and fell on them. Her flat smelt of dead flowers. When she had seen him she had stretched out her arms for him, the very picture of a long-lost mother, and he had felt six years' worth of needing to be hugged arrive in his chest. He had looked at her heaving bosom beneath her thin blouse and wanted to rest his head against it but he had remained rooted to the floor, each foot occupying a single tile. He watched his father awkwardly enter the gap in her arms that he had refused to fill. There was coffee in a percolator on the table. She poured some out for his father into a flowery mug which seemed too small for him, her hands fluttering. She kept saying someone called Brian would be back any minute and then smiling in a pretend happy way. His father kept looking away from her brown eyes, as if for hope, at another tower block just like hers where who knew what was invisibly happening. Fitch heard the carefree voices of children somewhere below. He wanted to be one of them, to be included in their game. His mother gave him a drink, forgetting that orange squash made him wheezy. It seemed that she found it hard to look at him, which he put down to guilt.

When they started looking through documents and letters he slipped away, carefully leaving his orange squash on the worktop. The other rooms were bare, except for a vast television and some matching black furniture. He looked at a few photos in a display cabinet and then he went over to the window and absorbed the faded-looking panorama until it was time to go. She did not leave what she was doing to come and talk to him. When it came to saying goodbye he did allow her to kiss him, just once. He was surprised by the softness of her lips, like the brush of the wings of a bird. And then on the way back in the train it had been dirty and grey and uncomfortable and hard to breathe in the smoking carriage which was the only place where they could find seats. His father had slept or closed his eyes anyway and Fitch had decided that this was the end of all those dreams he'd started having when he found out she was alive, about her coming back and living with them and all that happy families crap, as his father would have said. So she was dead in a way and this was how he had tried to think of her ever since. In the flat he had seen a photo of her cradled in the arms of a tall man with a black moustache like a circus master. She was dressed up and glamorous looking and she seemed happy. He thought, I must try to accept that, although I am unhappy, she is happy with the circus master, Brian, but then he thought of her sitting at the table, of her eyes and her hands, and knew that she was not. He loved his father then, for trying to save her. He could see now that this had been a hero's mission. He could see his father's turned head reflected in the train window. His eyes were open after all and he was watching the landscape with flicking eyeballs that seemed to say going, going, gone.

A bus arrived near the church. He got on it, not sure for a few moments whether he was still going in the opposite direction to Illerwick, but then when they were out on the open road he knew that they were. Here were windswept trees and dry stone walls and little groups of bungalows and caravan parks. He would get off quite soon because he remembered there was a way that you could cut through over some fields to Breakers Point. The bus didn't go down the road that had a car park at the end. In the summer all this area would be busy with cars and ice-cream vans and the car park would be manned by students in little temporary booths. He was still in familiar territory. He had wanted to come here ever since he had found out what had happened to Gabriel Vye. This was the way he must have come, on foot. Fitch wondered if anyone had seen him. He'd never known anyone who had died, if you could call it knowing. He'd seen him in church quite often. The Christmas before last, the Vyes had taken some kids carol singing. He remembered Miss Vye that day. She had been wearing a white fluffy hat and matching mittens. It was an outfit that would have looked stupid on anyone but her. He remembered that he had found out that her brother's name was Gabriel and he kept being conscious of it whenever it came up in the words of the carols. He had a deep voice, though, not angelic at all. You could see the resemblance between the two of them, except his hair was brown instead of fiery red. He'd seen him in the summer a few times, too, mowing the lawn or doing some job on the outside of their house. He never said hello but he had a way of giving you a wry smile, which made you feel you knew him better than you did.

He had seemed such a sturdy person. Fitch looked at his wrist where he held it against the glass of the bus window, supporting his head which suddenly felt very heavy. The sun was shining through the transparent skin, showing up the veins like a network of roots or the branches of winter trees. He thought of how, if the bus crashed, a piece of glass could cut through his flesh like butter. FRAGILE it said on the packages that his father would sometimes get in the post. Once, when he was younger, he had asked his father what it meant and he had said that inside the packages were plants that would snap in two unless you were careful. Just like you or me, he had said, sensitive plants that we are.

When he got off the bus he found that he remembered the way well enough. Everyone knew the way to Breakers Point. Everyone came to Breakers Point at some time in their lives. He went towards the car park, across a playing field with a children's playground in it. He marvelled at how children could be so happy with just a few metal climbing bars and a set of swings. He heard their shrieks of laughter and excited screaming, saw the mothers huddled in little groups, smoking. It doesn't take much, he thought, feeling very different from when he had come here in the past, when his mother had still been around and he had always begged to go on the swings before going down to the beach. He walked briskly along the cliff path. The sea today was, in the words of his father, as blue as a cornflower. He sat down and rested and thought of Gabriel Vye and the fact that this is where it had all happened. He was seen, he remembered that now. Not from here, but from the beach. There was a quote in the *Echo*. A man walking his dog had seen something in the air. That was how he came to be found so quickly. Fitch remembered the man had said at first he thought it was a bundle of old clothes being chucked off the edge of the cliff.

He felt his mind running out of control again. It kept doing this to him, lately. It happened to him sometimes when he was cycling along the road and a lorry went past or a farm machine. Thoughts of skulls being smashed or bones being crushed burst into his mind. The way a skull would shatter like an egg if it fell from a great height on to rocks. He threw a stone off the edge to steady himself. He remembered himself on the ramparts. He thought of Leo Spring and the way he had seen him crying the day Gabriel Vye had been found. He realised now that he couldn't have known then. He must have been crying because of her. He saw Miss Vye as still as a waxwork in a tall glass case like the ones they had at Porth Gwyn Museum, with Boase and Leo on the outside, pressing their faces, their fingers, against the glass and steaming it up. They couldn't touch her. He saw himself standing further off as a spectator. A mere boy. He had always hated Boase. He was cruel and nasty to Jimmy Rivers even though it was common knowledge that Jimmy's father beat him and locked him in a wardrobe, but now he hated him even more. Leo he could not hate. Even though Leo did love Miss Vye, he knew that she would never love him back, any more than she would love Boase. Anyone could see that.

Weeks and weeks had passed since Fitch had been to school. He thought of what would happen if he told the others what he had seen. He saw Pete making wanking gestures behind Boase's back. He thought, I will stay away. As long as it is just him in charge, then I will not go back.

22
MR BOASE

The pub is dark. The sun outside is strangely bright, still bright enough at four to make him blind as he pushes open the glass, whorl-panelled doors into the pub's red darkness. Boase stumbles against a chair, his rubber-soled Hush Puppies providing too much resistance against the varnished flagstones. A simultaneous burst of laughter. Boase stares fixedly ahead and sees the saggy outline of Jack Flagg behind the bar. Jack Flagg does not profess to know his regular tipple. He does not, thankfully, regard him as a regular despite his recent daily visits but Boase thinks he is, perhaps, rather surprised to be face to face yet again with someone who he always understood was not the drinking type, a chapel-goer no less. A person who had been known to lecture others on their behaviour. Who has been known to pick on his own son, Pete, at school.

'What'll I get you?' asks Jack.

'A pint of bitter,' he hears himself saying in a smaller voice than he intended. He holds out a note, which is nearly torn from his fingers by the gust from the opening door as some young lads from the building site across the road sweep in, roaring and joking. He will have taught them their tables once. They will recognise him, but he will not look. He will not look to see them roll their bullocks' eyes, whisper and mock or hear Mary Jones say, 'Talk about the pot calling the kettle black.'

He carries his pint carefully over to the corner table as he has done every evening for the last couple of weeks. He never spills a drop. He wants to be as far away as possible from the others, from the place near the pool table and the dartboard where there is always much banter and tomfoolery. He unfolds the *Telegraph*, which he has bought from Betty's shop next door. He pretends to do the crossword but only listens to the music on the jukebox that is always playing the same tunes, his emotions caught and suspended on every minor note of every sad song that the others choose. In every song it is her, it is him. He memorises the words and sings them silently in his head when he is alone.

Have they seen through his pretence? He will have one pint here, drain his glass with what he hopes is an air of finality, tightly folding his paper under his arm. He will walk smartly down the street in the direction of his house. Then he will go to The Lion on the edge of town, which is usually empty and where the landlady doesn't pry into the affairs of others. Then The Coach and Horses where he sits out of the way, in the snug, not much caring any more. Each pub is different, with its own particular ornaments and knick-knacks and smells but the décor is always the colour of hellfire and damnation and in the quiet times before the evening rush, everyone is always avoiding everyone else's eyes.

He will go the Londis shop on the way home and buy whisky. He will trudge back to his house in darkness – it is always dark these days by the time he reaches the estate, even though it is spring and the evenings are full of house martins and soft gold light and the sounds of children playing on their bikes. He never sits outside, although all the pubs have beer gardens, in case he is seen. Always inside. In a corner. Little Jack Horner. *Like Jack Horner in the corner . . . Your kisses are worth waitin' for, believe me . . . Ain't misbehavin' I'm savin' my love for you.* Last week, he started smoking again. Back to his old brand, Craven A, because they still make him feel like a film star when he's had a few. He lives on tins and bread and cheese. His larder is piled high with groceries that he has bought in the Londis shop, along with the whisky, to make the whisky look like an afterthought. Then he lies on his imitation velvet sofa and watches television: sitcoms at which he never laughs or smiles; docu-soaps about people he despises; crime programmes with scaremongering presenters in loud ties. He watches until he sees double. Sometimes he grows attached to snippets of songs he hears on adverts, which he waits in anticipation to hear again and again. His marking is piling up on his desk at school. He does not care. He thinks of her.

Sometimes he falls asleep on the sofa, waking in the early hours, startled by the harsh rasping of his own throat. He jolts awake, feeling the cold. He gulps water, staggers to his cold, functional bath-room with its solitary bar of Imperial Leather and takes painkillers in the faint light of the early dawn. He tries to block out the sound of birds and the dread of morning for another two hours until it is time to put on his uniform of blue blazer and grey trousers and go to school. In the playground he takes out his hangover on the smallest children who dart like sparks under his feet or swoop from one side of the playground to the other, squealing like gulls. He yells at them and they flee.

Sometimes he just watches the television with the sound turned off, lip reading, listening to the weather outside, thinking up phrases he would like to say to her, setting himself impossible problems, like the sum of his desire divided by the extent of her beauty. Impossible equations. Setting out the geometry of his feelings, the sharp angles of his pain against the statistical evidence that she wouldn't go near him even if he were the last man on earth. If he could have written poetry then he would have done but all that is out of his welkin.

Sometimes he vomits. Always neatly in the lava-tory and he always cleans the bowl afterwards with the pine disinfectant he keeps behind the pipe, or in the morning if he is too drunk to get the child-proof lid off the bottle. Although he sometimes falls and bangs his head, he prides himself on his control. He does not drink in the mornings. He swills out his mouth with Listerine. At school, he speaks from the corner of his mouth or turns away or keeps his distance. There have only been a few moments when he has lost the focus of what he was saying. When the world has seemed whirligig. Sometimes he has felt that the children had the power to outwit him and he has panicked and forgotten the answer but he has always turned the tables on them. He is finding it harder to maintain discipline. There are waves of talking that he cannot stop. He has resorted to desperate measures. He has made large boys stand on school chairs. He has thrown things, slammed the door and raised his voice. At least there is no Fitch and, as far as he can tell, he has not told the others.

One day she came back. It was the afternoon and he had set a test, which made them quiet and afraid. The classroom was silent, except for the movements of the children as they wriggled about and shuffled their papers. He saw her coming up the bank between the cherry trees, the blossom falling like snow. She was dressed in a pale mac that flew out behind her as she walked into the wind. Then she was in the corridor, her face quickly passing the small square window. She raised her hand. A gesture just for him. Panic jumped about inside him. The children had their backs to the window, their heads bent down. He put three Polos in his mouth at once and straightened his tie. When the test was over the children were limp and tired and some had gone to sleep. He collected their papers and dismissed them carelessly. In moments they were gone, out into the sunny afternoon. Melody watched them from the staffroom window, like a shepherdess counting her sheep, he thought, as he stood in the doorway watching her. Missing one.

23
FITCH

But one morning, Fitch did go back to school. The kids on the bus were impressed by his long absence. Their eyes appraised him admiringly as he lurched up the aisle to the coveted back seat. He indulged their loose badinage but inside he felt dread.

'You're in big trouble, mate,' they said.

'Vye'll have your guts for garters,' said Pete, his big, red, freckled face crinkled up with laughter.

No one mentioned Boase. To them, he was unimportant. Fitch feared an act of violence beyond his imagining, out of Miss Vye's sight.

They had English before break. Fitch couldn't concentrate because he was watching her. She looked thinner and paler than ever, her eyes a darker and more mysterious green. At the end of the lesson, she called him up to the desk.

'You've been away a long time, I hear.'

'Yeah.' He studied the grooves on the desk. He remembered then that this was where Boase had been sitting. She was sitting in the very chair.

'Have you brought a note?'

Fitch could only think, I have been to Breakers

Point. I have been to Breakers Point. He burned to get away, to be away from her, to not feel as though he had let her down when he hadn't.

In the end he said, 'My father can't write.'

But she suddenly seemed as though she didn't want to carry on talking to him.

'Well, you've got a lot of catching up to do,' she said, vaguely, twisting a strand of her hair around her finger like copper wire.

'No problemo.' He smiled at her encouragingly but she was looking away towards the coast.

When he went out into the corridor he saw Boase hovering by the noticeboard; it was still morning break and everyone was outside. He ran past him, realising in that moment that it was Boase who was scared of him. Boase waited until he was at the end of the corridor before he said, 'Don't run!' but it was obviously only for Miss Vye's benefit. Fitch turned and, checking that Miss Vye was still in the classroom, he held his hand aloft and made a V sign. Two first-years held the door open for him. Open Sesame.

24

VALENTINA

On the day of the school concert, Leo went down with flu. Valentina left him waving to her from an upper window, wanly. Fitch had gone on ahead, clutching his sheet music. The trees in the beech wood were full of a rushing wind that was somehow unearthly. And although in her heart she wanted to hang back, the wind urged her on and when she arrived at the school there were still groups of parents dawdling by the front entrance in the playground. Inside it was noisy and hysterical and everyone seemed to know each other. She squeezed in at the back, next to a round couple who smelt faintly of beer. They smiled at her, introduced themselves as Jack and Mary from The Crown and continued quietly nagging each other under their breath. She thought she heard them mention Melody but they could have been talking about the musical programme for all she knew. There were several women without coats still standing, who could have been teachers, and Valentina studied each one, trying to determine which could be Melody Vye. Neither Leo nor Fitch had actually described her and Valentina suddenly felt embarrassed that she would not know who to approach at the interval. She wouldn't have much time.

It went quieter. Then there was the sound of a woman's shoes tapping in the foyer and she swept in, her head held high. Valentina caught a flash of a pale cheekbone, a skein of burning-red hair as she walked down the aisle to the front row, a grey, male teacher shadowing her. There was a last glimpse of her face above the bobbing heads as she turned momentarily, before sitting, to smile and nod concisely at someone at the back whose job it was to turn off the house lights. The back curtains were squeakily drawn against latecomers, there was a hush and the concert began. She was beautiful.

The music teacher was large and passionate – Valentina could see why Fitch had avoided her like the plague. She wore a dress with chiffon sleeves that floated out of time to the bellows-like action of her arms but the back of her nodding head with its springing, steel-grey curls suggested she was not to be trifled with. Valentina glanced at the programme she had found on her seat and saw Fitch's name near the end. The first half was mainly singing – the junior choir did 'Oklahoma!' and then there were some solos; a girl with an operatic-sounding voice sang 'Ave Maria' and Fitch's friend Suzy performed 'Moon River' in the manner of Audrey Hepburn. The end of the first half was a small boy playing the *Trumpet Voluntary*. Valentina thought of poor Leo in bed. For the last week, before he got ill, he had been playing with the window open and she had listened to him as she weeded in between the flags on the terrace. It seemed obvious now that the garden scheme could never really happen in quite the way he had envisaged. Sitting in her loft at night, she tried to describe him in her journal. She made him into a character with a breaking heart. She made herself into another character who loved him.

At the interval the grey-haired male teacher with the flushed face was sternly manning a makeshift bar on two trestle tables in the foyer. Valentina saw Melody Vye standing in front of the tables and slipped in beside her. She smiled and Melody Vye smiled back, thinking they must know each other, exactly as Valentina had known she would.

She launched straight in. She said she was Leo Spring's gardener. She said she'd come to hear Fitch because Leo wasn't well.

'His gardener?'

She tried to say how good he was at teaching Fitch the piano, to tell her about the Grand Scheme taking place in the gardens of Beech House. It was hard to shout all this above the cacophony of voices and laughter and the sound of the orchestra tuning up for the second half. Valentina saw Fitch slinking past.

She tried again: 'He was so sad not to be able to come tonight.' She looked up into Melody Vye's face. Her eyes were the colour of green glass when the sea has worn it down.

'You should come up and see it. You wouldn't believe what we've done already.'

The headmistress's eyes were catching someone else's over her shoulder, telling them to ring the bell to say the interval was over. She smiled apologetically as she turned away.

Valentina went back to her seat. At least she had tried. Fitch's turn came. He walked stiffly to the front of the stage and bowed, which made the audience laugh. As he played the *Moonlight Sonata* Valentina walked around the gardens of Beech House in her head. Around every corner was Leo, his face against the leaves. She saw his face at the window tonight, smiling hopefully. It made her feel like crying.

Fitch bowed again at his applause and this time was taken seriously. As everyone left, she saw him with a man who must have been his father. The father had his arm round his shoulders. She heard a boy's voice call, 'Well done, Fitch, mate!' Valentina felt suddenly lonely. She saw Melody Vye a little way off, saying goodbye to some parents. She turned and waved to her. The headmistress raised a little white hand uncertainly in the dusk among the drifting faces.

25

MELODY

Gabriel is eight. Melody is ten and in charge of him but it is she who follows, cycling in his wake, over melting tarmac to the fields right at the end of the peninsula. Dragging her bike across the lumpy grass behind him. Scratching her bare legs on thistles. But she wants to go. She wants to see them as much as he does. He gets on his bike on the flat part and so does she, afraid of losing him, of letting him out of her sight which would mean breaking her promise to Daddy. It feels as though he is being drawn away from her on an invisible rope. She calls to him to wait but he doesn't hear her. Or doesn't want to. They come to a little gully where a dried-up stream meets the shingle and they ditch their bikes. They scramble up to the cliff path which is more of a sheep path really. Freed of their bikes, they relax and allow themselves to look about, to see the sea with its miniature ships balancing on the horizon.

Gabriel is still the leader. He is running now, scattering sheep who seem to race blindly off the edge of the cliff, but this is only an illusion. She follows him around the curve of the cliffs. When they come to gullies he springs from rock to rock, sure-footed in his Startrite sandals. She wishes she wasn't wearing flip-flops.

It's the first time this year that they have come to the cove. It started last year when Melody found it by accident. She had taken him without telling anyone and he had got stung by a bee and she had got into trouble. No one had listened. Then it became a secret. They always pray that they will see no one, that they will not meet anyone from Illerwick. Sometimes they see walkers in long socks with plastic-coated maps around their necks. Gabriel ignores them. She smiles falsely at the wives. Gabriel has stopped. She waits, a few paces behind. He gives her a thumbs-up signal. He inches towards the edge of the cliff, then lies down flat on his stomach. She creeps up and lies behind him on the sheep-bitten grass, checking for droppings and thistles first. They look out together, side by side, spying between the stems of scabious and thrift. At first she doesn't see anything. Then she does. One, two, three, four, five. It is a whole family, their inky eyes peering nosily out above the water. Gabriel is up on his knees. Then, one by one, the seals clamber out to bask on the rocks.

26
VALENTINA

The day after the concert at five o'clock Valentina followed the beacon of Melody's hair through the town. She hung far enough back for Melody not to be aware of her. For a while, she thought the male teacher from the concert seemed to be following but after a few moments he disappeared somewhere near The Crown. As Melody approached the river, Valentina took a shortcut through the churchyard so that she arrived opposite Melody's house just as Melody was opening the gate.

'Would you like some lilac?' she said, holding up a plastic bag with lilac flowers shooting up out of it. 'Leo remembered how much you liked the lilacs at Beech House.'

Melody seemed tired. She looked straight through the gaps in the lilac branches and into Valentina's eyes. Valentina looked back into Melody's. She turned and went in and Valentina followed her through the open door.

The house was very dark inside. There were internal wooden shutters which had obviously been closed since the morning. Melody did not open them. She led the way into a shady garden that sloped down to a stretch of the river, screened by a curtain of weeping willows. She stood looking at everything with her back to Valentina for a few moments, then she sat down and Valentina came and sat near her on a stone bench. Melody didn't offer her anything to drink and she remained silent so Valentina put the bag of lilac down against the side of the bench. The movement seemed to startle her.

She said quietly, 'I don't feel anything for him.'

And Valentina saw that it was true, that she didn't love him.

'I suppose I might have let him think that I did, once. When we were very young, perhaps. I didn't think it mattered.'

There didn't seem much that Valentina could say so she didn't say anything. Some willow leaves blew about on the ground near their feet.

'I can't love anyone at the moment. I just need time to grieve for Gabriel.'

Valentina thought what it must have been like for her to lose her brother. She thought of Jonathan far away and imagined him being sucked up by a gigantic wave in Unawatuna.

'I'm sorry,' she said, 'about what happened to your brother.'

Melody smiled. 'You don't look like a gardener,' she said.

'You don't look like a headmistress. What do gardeners look like?' Or writers, she thought.

Melody smiled again. 'I can't believe that you've

really managed to do much with the gardens at Beech House.'

'I think you'd be surprised if you came to have a look,' said Valentina, confident that she wouldn't. 'I've got Fitch to help me, you know. It's his Saturday job.'

'I hope you and Leo are not to blame for all this time he's had off school. It's slave labour, if you ask me.'

'I think there's something else on his mind. It's not the music and it's not the job.'

Melody didn't say anything. Valentina picked up the lilac. She wanted to go home. She wasn't sure who she was supposed to be any more. But when she looked at Melody she saw that she was crying. She sat down next to her and put her arm round her shoulders. She let the weight of Melody's grief fall against her chest.

When Valentina left it was growing dark. On her way through the town, she thought she saw a meandering figure ahead of her on the pavement that might or might not have been the grey-haired teacher. As she walked through the dark grounds of Beech House she felt frightened about the situation she had got herself into. Leo's plans were growing wildly out of control but no progress was being made. The only good news was that Betty in the shop had told her that Patrick the gardener was still alive after all and in the old people's home, but she was not sure how much use that would be. As she passed the lighted window of the library she wondered whether she should go in and talk to Leo now. She looked at the back of the red chair and imagined his shrunk figure inside it, love-eaten. She turned to walk across the stable yard but then she smelt his smoke and she saw that he was leaning in the archway leading to the kitchen garden. He had been waiting for her to come back.

'Come on. Tell me what she said.' He started walking along the path to the orangery as though he were running away from the words that she might say.

Valentina thought, now I am going to have to lie again to this man who should never be lied to. The air felt warm and soft as she followed him through the blue dusk to the orangery where he had been coming lately to teach Fitch the guitar. When Fitch went home, he would light candles and mope there and write mysteriously in a dark green notebook.

'How was she?' was all that he asked.

'Fine,' she said. 'Missing Gabriel. She cried about Gabriel.'

'Yes,' he said, 'I expect she did.' And then there was silence.

27
MELODY

There was a face in Melody's dream. The face of a
girl whose eyes looked into hers. She dreamed that
she laid her cheek against the soft skin of the girl's
breasts. She half woke up. She ran her hand across
her own breasts and felt the nipples rise. She stroked
her stomach and made goose pimples. She sat up
with a jolt. She laid her hands outside the sheets. I
have been dreaming about another woman, she
thought. I must be going mad.

28

VALENTINA

Valentina was thinking about Leo. She was lying in bed, her mouth, her lips, resting gently against her forearm where the little hairs scratched the thin skin of her lips almost like stubble. She was thinking what it would be like to kiss him. She was rubbing her lips across her arm, thinking about his forearms, which had darkened slightly in the sun, a tangle of gold thread running up and down them. She felt that there was something edible about them. She thought of licking them and imagined their salty taste. She was thinking about the roughness of the hairs against her tongue, imagining the hairs tickling her bare skin as he encircled her, as he grasped her in his arms. She reached for her journal.

29

VALENTINA

Valentina and Jonathan are riding home from school in a trishaw. They are seven. A rosary swings hypnotically back and forth in front of the tiny windscreen. Tinsel is sellotaped around the edge of the dashboard. There is a picture of Jesus. Valentina likes tinsel. It looks better here than at home. It looks shinier, more sparkly. She likes the way it doesn't have to be Christmas here to have tinsel. The rain started at the usual time. They say: Rain. Rain. Don't go away. They like the rain. They find it dramatic. It's drumming fast now. The banana leaves are getting torn. One road is a river of brown and they can't go down it. The driver swings round, quacking his horn and they go rattling down another street. He knows this city like the palm of his hand, says Jonathan. She looks at her own palm with all its lines and squiggles. She imagines Colombo like an enormous palm holding them precariously in this storm, cupping them out of danger. They have changed into their flip-flops for the journey and it's a good job because their feet are getting wet now. They hold on to their plimsolls in their red cloth pump-bags with their names embroidered on by Nanna in England in yellow chain stitch. The driver stops and pulls down the plastic sheets so they are snug inside like in a tent but there are still plenty of gaps to look through.

The balloon man was not on the corner today. Every day she waits to see the balloon man who makes animals out of bending balloons and who even wears balloon ears around his head, which makes her think of him as a giant rabbit. Neither she nor Jonathan has ever asked for a balloon. Listen to that thunder! says Jonathan in a typical, boy-like way and she says it's only the gods moving their furniture around like Nanna would say. She imagines blue gods like she saw on a temple, with multiple, pliable limbs like octopuses moving their furniture carelessly with flicks of their wrists, forever dissatisfied with their new arrangements. Neither of them feels frightened of thunderstorms any more. They know this without asking each other. There was a time, once, when they were both frightened and they knew this too without saying anything. Then Valentina would sit on the end of Jonathan's bed and hold on to his feet under the bedclothes as if they were a tiller and she was steering them safely through the wild waters and floods of the night.

They stop in a queue and there is no way for the driver to get round it. He looks exasperated and says something they don't understand and then catches their eyes in the mirror, smiling apologetically, tilting his head. He has a flashy smile that

Valentina warms to. She thinks of him as being a bit like a pirate. Because they have stopped, they dare to lift the plastic sheet and look out. Even in the rain their two little matching fair heads cause a storm. Someone points and laughs and smiles. Jonathan tilts his head back to eat the rain and makes them laugh even more. So she does the same, only on the other side. Then the driver does it and they all laugh. Even the crows on the red, tiled rooftops are laughing. They like the driver. His name is Kumarasiri. He is the same driver they have every day. Every day he is waiting for them at the end of their drive. Every day Mum sees them off from an upstairs window in the cool of the house behind the diamonds of a grille and gives a little wave and they wave back.

When they get home today, Mum will sit with them while they eat their lunch but she won't have anything because she isn't feeling very well again. They are more adventurous with food now. Valentina hears her mother telling her friends on the phone that they have become more adventurous with food. She likes this idea, as though they are exploring a giant country of *seeni sambol* and egg hoppers and chillis. She imagines a Sri Lanka made entirely of food. When she sees lorries go by carrying mountains of pineapples she thinks that it really is. At first they turned their noses up at everything. Dolma, their cook, was very anxious about this. She tempted them with little morsels, a little pineapple here, a red banana there, a few rambutans in their laps when they weren't looking. Now they have practically forgotten about English food, except for the spicy chips they have at the swimming club but these don't really count because they don't taste anything like English chips anyway. Now they sit, their chins only just up to the edge of the table in a room full of heavy rainforest-tree furniture, with the fan turning over and over them, listening to their mother telling them she and their father are going out again and they roll their terrible eyes like the Wild Things. She and Dad are going to the Nicholsons' for dinner. Tommy Nicholson is in their class. He is Jonathan's best friend, not counting her.

When it clears up a bit, they will go to the swimming club and dive and dive until their eyes are red and their noses are streaming snot. They like swimming in the rain. Jonathan says he's singing in the rain, just singing in the rain. What a glorious feeling, he's happy again. She will push up the mouldy cap that they make her wear because of her long, yellow hair, and lie back and feel the warm rain and look at it all coming down and try to remember what it felt like to go swimming in England indoors under a roof at the local baths. Afterwards they will sit at a white metal table under a big green-and-white-striped umbrella, their legs dangling down, and drink bottles of 7-Up because they are seven, and Mum will put down her papers and smile and look pleased with them. Then Dad will miraculously appear from nowhere and order the special spicy chips as a treat along with his Lion lager and smoke a cigarette. He will ask them test questions to see if they have been concentrating at school but they are always the same ones so they know the answers and then they will climb, almost dry, into the back of Dad's car which will be steamy hot in the back until they get the air-conditioning going.

In the evening, Martha Crawford will come over to baby-sit. She's a teenager who goes to the senior part of their school and she brings over her own tapes and plays them on Mum and Dad's stereo and lets them stay up and dance while she smokes and leans back in the long planter's chair on the verandah. When it is time to go to bed she acts like she's ignoring them but she watches them through cat eyes and if they put a foot wrong she yowls at them so they are a little afraid of her and this is how she likes it. Once, a boy came who she said was her friend but they didn't seem to talk much. Jonathan called her and they crept up to the roof and they had a bird's-eye view of them kissing. They looked like snakes. Then they must have heard her parents' car and the night-watchman go to open the gate because the boy ran away into the garden and disappeared.

On other days after school, they play old-fashioned games like Old Maid and Snakes and Ladders and Jackstraws sitting on the windowsill. England seems far away. Their parents are different here too. They clink ice into heavy-bottomed glasses and drink Chelsea gin and sit by the fan and seem dazed by the softly swaying banana leaves and strange birds in the garden. The sun sets behind huge clouds that make fantastic shapes like hot air balloons and castles and palaces. School doesn't seem like hard work. The school building is made out of an old house and they spend a long time playing dusty, imaginary games behind the whitewashed walls of a schoolyard that used to be a garden. The other things, the things that happen in the old, dark, heavy classrooms with the sticky polished floors, they don't often understand. There is always the thick, musty smell of other children's bodies like the hot breath of a dog on their faces. Sareeka always understands school things far better than Valentina does. Sareeka is the best at Kandyan dancing, better than all the other girls put together. Sareeka's father is an astronaut, which greatly interests Jonathan, but they have never actually seen him.

30

VALENTINA

The old people's home was outside the town, a modern, Spanish-style bungalow that had been added to and added to until it seemed to stretch for ever behind itself into the pale green sea of sheep-bitten grass and scraggy gorse. A nurse showed Valentina into the lounge and pointed out Patrick. He was sitting in front of a large, double-glazed window looking absorbed, as if he was watching a film. His armchair, of the same design as Leo's but with a brown nylon cover stretched over it like a complicated bathing costume, dwarfed him. In his hand, balanced against his thin, bird's chest, he grasped a white cup and saucer that seemed somehow to be weighting him down, preventing him from floating off into the next world like a piece of thistledown. Valentina sat down beside him. She looked out through the window and saw a sky full of tall, pale grey clouds. Almost imperceptibly, the clouds were shifting. The crows that splashed their wings across the clouds, both near and far, were like the black flecks on an old film reel. She looked at the old man's profile and saw the boy he had grown from. He tore his eyes from the sky for a few seconds and smiled and nodded as though she came and sat there every day. Maybe he thought he knew her. Maybe pretending to know everyone was a good disguise for forgetfulness. Valentina was pleased. It made things easier because she could just start asking about the garden without giving any explanations of herself.

He said he knew it like the palm of his hand. He turned over his own arthritic hand that would never again be unfurled and looked at it blankly. Beech House he spoke of only as 'thowze'. He had gone there at the age of fourteen, sent by his parents, and had never worked anywhere else. He paused between sentences to get his breath but drew attention away from his lack of breath by making it look as though he had been distracted by peripheral sounds which his eighty-eight-year-old ears could never have heard, such as the wheels of the tea trolley squeaking or the unfolding of a newspaper on the other side of the room.

Valentina had an encyclopaedia with large colour plates of garden flowers and plants. She put it in his lap and let him leaf through it. His hands acted as though the glossy pages were made of glass. He weighed the book up and down and laughed in disbelief that a book could be so large. He made slow progress through it, lingering over every variety of geranium he had ever grown, pursing his lips and looking up so she would know it was one of his and could write it down in her notebook. She showed him a plan. She let him trace the stub of his finger over his old territory, up and down the paths where he had wheeled his barrow for sixty years.

'Down this walk,' he said, 'I grew London Pride.'

He identified the roses in the rose garden, the names like a ghostly roll-call: Madame Alfred Carrière, Bobbie James, Penelope, Félicité, Constance Spry.

'They are all still there,' she said, bringing them to life.

The herbaceous borders would all have to be replanted and by the breathy names and his pointings she was able to piece together a sort of jigsaw of the beds. She drew shapes on a piece of paper and he pointed and she wrote the names of the plants in the blank spaces. Later she would draw it neatly and show it to Leo. She felt excited.

He kept calling her Glyn but, after a while, she realised that Glyn was his son. He did casual work in the gardens at Pengelli Castle. Later she phoned Glyn up and arranged for him to come and rotavate the vegetable garden and mow the lawns with his sit-on mower.

31

MELODY

At all the times during the day when Melody wasn't concentrating on the task in hand, she thought of the girl, Valentina. When she was not teaching, she looked out of her office window at the empty, rain-blackened playground where crisp packets blew like bright phantoms and seemed to see only the girl's heart-shaped face coming towards her, seeking her out amongst the crowds of other, familiar faces who had brought her no comfort. She is my saviour, she thought, my illumination after the dark days of winter. When Melody sat at her computer screen waiting for things to happen, she thought simply, this is the one I have wanted.

She was an unusual person, but Melody liked unusual people. There was something awkward about her, as if she didn't quite fit into her own skin, as if she were disguising something and this intrigued Melody. Leo would not have noticed. Leo was blind. Valentina had trembled when she spoke of him. She was in awe of him. But when she had spoken of Gabriel's death something had happened between them. Out of Valentina's blue eyes came a feeling, something, which felt like a rope that she could use to pull herself to safety. Every time she thought of her, she felt a flutter inside, a little trill of heartbeats. And at night, when she lay in her dark house listening to the river racing coldly in its bed, she thought of the younger woman's firm embrace, the feeling of her own ear against the hard breastbone, the strong, regular breathing against the crown of her head.

The end of the day came and the children left. She walked down the corridor. She looked in at Mr Boase's classroom to see if he was still there. There was such a mountain of books on his desk that she had to go right inside the room to see whether he was behind them or even underneath them. She imagined him walling himself in against the children, constructing a fortress of Maths books behind which to hide. But there was no one there. She glanced at the confusion of papers and knew that her absence had been too much of a burden. The room smelt of bad breath. Outside, it was the kind of warm, blowy evening when she would have liked to sit on the garden swing at Beech House.

She knew Valentina would be doing the same things that she herself had always done at Beech House in the past. She could imagine her in the garden, walking up and down the paths and terraces, except that now it would all have been changed. All that evening her mind worked on schemes that would bring them together. Some of them involved going to Beech House and some of them didn't. It was a madness that grew inside her like the tendrils of a voracious climbing plant. She stood looking through the window at her own garden, a square of tangled green. She chopped vegetables with her mother's old sharp knife and made enough soup for a week and scrubbed and scrubbed at the kitchen floor where the smudges of Gabriel's footprints still left their mark and could not be eradicated.

When she couldn't sleep she got dressed and went into the garden. She was trying to still herself. The garden seemed magic, the passion flower a bank of stars. She climbed the willow tree and slid down onto the other side and plunged through the darkness and through the beech wood with no fear, and in that time she walked through her own dreams. The dry roar of the threshing leaves and spattering down of twigs and beechmast did not frighten her. She ran along the wide, empty path. The owls stretched the skeins of their voices between the high branches, floating by on silent wings. The sheep coughed in the blackness. When she got near the house she started creeping. She took off her shoes and picked her way around the edges of the gravel drive. The sharp stones hurt her feet. She could hear the garden all around her invisibly breathing, the leaves rubbing together like thousands of hands. She went to the stable but the light was off and all was silent. She walked around the house and looked in at the library. There were some lamps on and light pooled around the dark, upholstered furniture like afternoon sun through branches. She went round the side of the house, where a heavy-headed rose brushed her cheek. The grass under her feet was cool and wet. She went towards the orangery. She was on all fours on the terrace above it. She looked in through the skylight. There was music. Leo, playing the guitar. Candlelight. She looked down on their heads like God. She heard the soft murmur of Leo saying something and then laughter, a ripple of notes. Hers. She ran away.

32

VALENTINA

Valentina was watching Leo. She was watching particularly his hands, his arms where his shirtsleeves were rolled up. She was supposed to be listening to a love song he had been writing for Melody. He'd tried to get Fitch interested in singing it, but he had refused scornfully so Leo was left to sing it himself. He was concentrating on the tune, which he was playing on the guitar. Sometimes he forgot the words and he just hummed and smiled at her for those bits as if the words didn't matter. He seemed relaxed, lately, as though nothing mattered. Only when Melody was mentioned by name did he suddenly become sad. It was the trigger of her name.

Valentina was writing about him. At night she had been sitting up late in her high loft bed drafting and redrafting a story in which she mourned the loss of her Little Mermaid hair and made Leo into a myopic prince who could not see the wood for the trees. She had found an old black typewriter that still worked in a junk room in the stable yard and she typed out a different version of the story every morning before the day's work in the garden began.

33
MELODY

Melody thought that she might bump into Valentina by chance. On the pavement outside school, in the supermarket, on the bus. When she was weeding her front garden in the dry spells she looked hastily over her shoulder in case she was being watched. She walked slowly past the windows of all the pubs. In The Crown she waved to Jack. In The Coach and Horses she was surprised to see Mr Boase. She waved to him but her eyes were scanning the rest of the room, hunting the dark red corners for the girl called Valentina. She found a reason to go to the garden centre and skulked among the statues and the rows of pots in the rain, waiting for anoraked figures to turn round. She went swimming at the new leisure centre. The blood-temperature water seemed not the same element as the dark sea that had taken Gabriel. The illusion created by the blue tiled floor fooled her and it seemed that the shifting mosaic of light on the water was part of a dream. She heard her breaths quicken as she swam faster and faster, more and more lengths towards a picture in her mind that led nowhere, the distance travelled wasted. Valentina and Gabriel see-sawed in her thoughts: happiness and sadness, pleasure and pain.

Then the days brightened suddenly and pulled the dark veil of her thoughts away, blinding her against her own guilt for moments at a time. She went walking, her eyes always searching the horizon for a speck of a person that would resolve itself into Valentina. Then the sharp sounds of the grass whipping her legs would take her back to the time when she and Gabriel were children, to all the years of her past that could never be taken away. The trees, the hedges, were all the same. Not as tall as then – everything shrank as you got older – but the gaps in the branches of the trees could have held Gabriel's voice, a leftover autumn leaf out of season, part of the mulch under foot, the sounds of his bicycle spokes suspended, web-like, in the hedge. The knots in the bark trapped the air they had once breathed. Rain scattered the sun. The ruts in the lane had only deepened, their parallel channels straightening the lines of her steps. Nettles scorched her fingers if she lost control of them. The wind blew hot and cold.

At the seal cove, the big boulders had shrunk. The sea had licked them down to size as easily as if they were black ice-creams in the short space of years. The wind blew there as hard as ever, shifting the powdery sand on the high part of the beach, changing the look of things subtly, disguising the pattern that was there before. Her gaze roamed over the grey horizon looking and looking for the black beads of the seal heads.

She breathed in. The wind cleansed her. Valentina. She loved her name. She breathed it out into the wind and it came back to her. She sucked it into her mouth and rolled it around her tongue, letting it loll there. But Gabriel was dead. She was too cowardly to go to Breakers Point but she was here still looking out into the same sea that swallowed him, the sea into which he fell through the air and where like the seals he became different – in his element. She saw his skin under water as white as a shell, his hair a strange kind of brown seaweed. She saw him as a merman, transformed.

The next day she went into the library and she saw her. She saw her and dropped her books. Valentina did not look up. She was in the poetry section. Melody felt herself gliding over the parquet floor towards her. From the back she looked like a boy. She looked almost like Fitch.

'A poetic gardener?' she said but it came out mockingly. She was afraid.

'Oh, yes. This is fertiliser for my brain.'

Melody's eyes filled embarrassingly with tears. This kept happening to her. But she was right. There was more to Valentina than met the eye. She said, 'Is this where your real interests lie?'

Valentina seemed to take a deep breath. She blushed. She told her she wanted to be a writer, that she wrote stories and poems. She said she found Illerwick inspiring. Then she looked as though she wished she had never spoken of such things.

Melody thought, this is my chance. She told Valentina that she should come to supper and read her something she had written. She said, 'You know that English is my subject?'

Valentina looked as though she would rather die. She said, 'I think it's closing time.'

They stood before the tallest bookcase. Melody could feel the heat of the sunlight. The shadow-structure of the window frame enclosed them. Mrs Dugdale was clanking around by the door. Valentina went to take out her books and Melody followed. Mrs Dugdale hovered between them, conducting her elaborate ceremony of stamps and cards.

'Come and find me after school one day?' Melody said.

34
FITCH

Fitch walked through a blur of insects and mead-owsweet to Beech House. The countryside had suddenly become thick and green and enclosing. Only reluctantly, between the trees and hedges, did it fade hazily away in gradations of green to the edges of the blue hills inland and merge with the sea mist in the other direction. Pete, Dave, Suzy and the others had gone to the beach but he had not. The job and his piano lesson had been good excuses. But things were changing: up until now, the boys and the girls at school had stayed separate. Suzy and he had broken the mould by being friends but this was not enough to make a real impact. Now, some of the boys and some of the girls seemed to be making an uneasy alliance. In the warm, light evenings the boys would mosey down to the old railway bridge and swing dangerously across the weir on a piece of old rope, a relic from past generations of Illerwick. Then the girls would arrive, as if by chance, and the atmosphere would get edgy. Water fights would start. There would be a lot of raucous screaming and dares. Now they had started going to the beach.

Last Sunday, when it was hot and humid, they had gone to Porth Gwyn on their bikes and hung around. He'd never done this much before. He had always been an outsider, never really part of Pete's group. He did not know why things were changing now, unless it was because of Suzy. Suzy was the only one who really talked to him but he was finding it more and more difficult to talk back. He never touched her, though he wanted to. Some of the other girls draped themselves over the boys' shoulders or instigated playfights. She did not. It was because they were already friends. The shape of her body had changed as though it had been secretly ripening beneath her school uniform for a whole year. Her sun-bathed skin was turning browner every day and the down on her body was whitening. He watched her flirting with the others, dancing and showing off, balancing on her bike so that everyone could see her knickers. He looked away. He could not make jokes and comments like Pete. He watched her flirting with Dave but saw the way her eyes flicked back to where he was sitting or searched for him on the edge of the group. It had become a joke now. Everyone knew that she had a crush on him. All he knew was that he avoided touching her, avoided being with her more and more and that there was a fear constantly in his mind that he would not know what to do, that he would only do something wrong and she would turn away and that they would all laugh. She was the smallest of the girls, but the bravest. When the girls went off by themselves, giggling, he was relieved.

They would go higher up the beach and lie on their fronts with their bikini tops off beneath the sunless sky, always one step ahead, moving things on, taking the risks. Some of the girls had flat chests but it didn't seem to make any difference. The boys glanced over casually, disguising the fact that they were riveted. He was terrified of what he felt. He lay hidden, face down, pretending to sleep, laughing at jokes he only half understood, doing everything the others did, praying the thunder would turn into rain and they would have to go home.

35

VALENTINA

It was raining when Valentina went to the school. The male teacher she had seen at the concert was coming out of the entrance.

He said, 'The school is closed,' as though he was bringing the heavy door shut against her face.

'Is Melody still here?' she said, ignoring what he had said, looking not into his eyes but along the dark shadows behind his glasses which pointed down to the corners of his mouth.

'Miss Vye will be leaving the premises shortly,' he said carefully. 'If you wish to see her, you will have to make an appointment on Monday.'

She looked behind him, through the green squares of the reinforced door, and saw the dark cut-out of the headmistress.

Her voice came floating from the end of the corridor: 'It's all right. I asked her to meet me here. This is Valentina. She's a writer. Valentina, this is Mr Boase, my deputy head.' Seeing his expression of irritation, she added, 'My linchpin,' but behind his back she rolled her eyes and smiled secretly at Valentina. His face relaxed into a childish smile but they didn't shake hands with each other. The moment had come and gone.

'Well, if that's the case,' he said and held the door a little wider so she could squeeze through. But he must have stood and watched and waited as the two of them walked along the long, green corridor because it was not until they reached the end of it that she heard the door bang shut.

Valentina felt uneasy. The school, now empty and childless, seemed a hostile place. She thought of the trials of Fitch, of his mysterious unhappiness. The heaviness of Melody's office, the darkness of the furniture, only made her seem lighter and more delicate. She shut down the computer. They watched Mr Boase walk across the playground and disappear into the rain.

'I'm sorry you've got all wet. I imagined it would be a lovely day when you came and I was going to suggest we went for a walk first. Never mind, I've got my umbrella – we'll just go back to my house.'

Valentina pulled the hood of her waterproof tightly around her face. 'I don't need an umbrella,' she said. The bag with her stories in was hurting her hand.

They didn't talk much as they walked along because the rain got harder, drumming monsoon-like on the taut nylon of Valentina's hood and on Melody's big umbrella. Jonathan flashed into her mind, a fork of lightning. She hardly looked where she was going, blundering through the rain, watching only her feet pacing in front of her, walking through all the puddles and never around them. Melody's will was too strong. Leo's will was too strong. She was caught between them. From under her umbrella, Melody called out to anyone they passed. Valentina bowed her head.

Valentina thought of the moment when they met in the library. She had seen Melody through the window. She had thought, this is the opportunity that Leo has been waiting for. Her back had been turned but she knew she would be found. She had heard Melody's books slap onto the floor. She had heard Melody's voice falling like a ripe plum at her feet. She studied the diagonal lines of the parquet before answering. She tried to think, this is what Leo wants. She had turned and looked at the hard, white marble face of Melody Vye, the freckles like pinpricks. She had seemed stretched to the very limits of herself. What would it take, Valentina had thought, as she had answered Melody's sharp questions, for her to jump off a cliff?

Inside Melody's house, the shutters had not been closed but the rain and the darkened sky still made the room shadowy when they got inside. Melody had left her sipping wine, standing looking out at the bedraggled garden and the river but Valentina followed her into the kitchen and tried to talk about Beech House and all the clearing and changing of things that was happening. Melody seemed to disapprove of the changes as though she wanted to stop Time.

'What was it like when you knew it?' Valentina asked her and in her mind she meant, then. When you were hardly younger than I am now. Tell me what it was like. What was Leo like, then?

'Well, I remember the fountain. I fell in it one night and had to be rescued. I think it was turned off after that.'

Valentina saw her, her wet clothes clinging to her slender limbs, the scales of the moonlight on her, the bright coils of her hair darkened.

'I don't know. I think I liked the way it was all overgrown. There was always a place to hide. There was a gardener there then. I think we always got in his way.'

Valentina decided not to tell her about Patrick for the time being. She'd already asked him about Melody. 'A flirt,' was all he would say.

'We didn't really pay much attention to the flowers. We just lazed around or played tennis.'

Valentina had not paid much attention to the tennis courts.

'Is he good at tennis?' she asked.

'Who, Leo? Oh, no! Leo didn't play; it was just Gabe and I. Leo is not really a tennis person.'

Valentina saw him watching, waiting. Always on the sidelines as she was now. She knew that Gabriel had somehow eclipsed him. The mysterious Gabriel that she had never seen. They looked out into the garden, now washed clean and dripping.

'He still loves you as much as he did then,' said Valentina quietly.

Melody banged the oven door shut. 'He's been telling you everything, hasn't he. Did he tell you about New Year's Eve? You know it probably drove Gabriel over the edge.' There was an awkward pause and then she carried on. 'There was never anything between us. I don't love him. I never did. I liked him, yes, but now he's made it – all of this has made it – impossible even to be friends.' Her eyes blurred. 'I know he's perfectly nice. I just don't love him.'

'I mean, he really loves you,' said Valentina. 'He will die if you don't love him back.' But then she thought that she shouldn't have talked about anyone dying.

'He won't die.' Melody went out of the room.

She came back a few minutes later and, framed in the doorway, through the steam of the potatoes she was carrying, her hair curled by the rain, her face flushed by the heat of the oven, she was more beautiful than ever before.

Valentina felt angry. She said, 'I just don't understand it.' She meant how anyone could not love him. 'I don't know how he will bear the rejection.'

'He will bear it.'

They ate. Valentina made some enthusiastic remarks about the food which Melody ignored.

Valentina was aware of the story in her bag. She looked around at the floor-to-ceiling bookshelves, at the furniture that Melody's parents had chosen once, or perhaps inherited. She thought, she is stuck here. Amongst her parents' things which have never been changed. She is as stuck in the mud as Leo.

'Now,' Melody was saying gently, 'Your story?'

Valentina took out her sheaf of papers. She did not know why she had told Melody about her writing. She had not even told Jonathan. The story was a private, individual thing, something pure, that belonged to her and now she was exposing it to the harsh light of Melody Vye's opinion. Her hands trembled. She wondered if she should tell her that the Little Mermaid had been the seed from which the story had grown or if this would make it seem childish. She wondered if Melody would be able to tell that this was her own love song to Leo.

They had not turned on the lights and the rain was making it darker and darker outside. The typed words shimmied on the page. Melody sat completely still in the shadows. Valentina heard her own voice faltering as she began to read. Melody listened. When Valentina finished reading she looked across at the other woman's face, at her shadowed eyes. She wanted her approval. She waited.

Then Melody said, 'It is the saddest story I have ever heard.'

In the end, that was all she said. She seemed to have gone into a sort of trance. Valentina decided not to read her the poems.

On the doorstep Melody took her hand. Her grasp was cool and firm.

'Did Leo ask you to play Cupid?'

'Yes,' she said, extricating her fingers.

'I'd like to hear more of your writing,' she said. 'You know, you could send that story to a magazine I know of.' Then she seemed to lose track of what she was saying.

Valentina felt confused. She opened the gate. A

car splashed past. She was halfway down the road before she realised she had left her story behind.

From then on, she disobeyed Leo and tried to avoid Melody. It was easy out in the open air. She'd see her in the distance, her hair flying out behind her, her pale face turning this way and that like a searchlight. Her eyes were always fixed on the horizon, never under her nose, or else she was dreaming, surrounded by a black cloud about to dissolve itself into rain.

The garden plans were becoming more and more complicated. The mixture of sun and rain had been perfect growing conditions and the weeds had taken over in the blink of an eye. She and Fitch battled endlessly against hogweed and nettles as tall as themselves and taller. Patrick's list of must-haves was growing ever longer. He kept remembering things as he pored over the giant plant encyclopaedia. Valentina feared it would crush him. Each plant he remembered was accompanied by a long and winding tale of how he first came by it as a boy and its exact requirements for optimum growth. He was exhausting himself. Valentina suspected this Scheherazade-like behaviour was so that she would keep coming and sitting by the big window in the old people's home, whiling away hours that she didn't have.

Life in Illerwick was tying her up in knots. As she listened to Patrick's scratchy voice and stared out into the mackerel skies at the gold jet streams of aeroplanes, she thought of Jonathan in Sri Lanka.

She thought, can I not just go and find him? But she knew she was too proud and that it was not what he wanted. She must make her own individual mark here. The garden was not enough. In the stable, she continued to concoct her stories and poems about Illerwick. She had disguised everything. Illerwick was Illerwick but it was not. The people, the main street, the blue hills that cut them off from the world were and were not. The garden was becoming two different gardens – the unwieldy, difficult project where things died or would not die and the garden in her mind, in her stories. She thought of the future garden in Leo's mind and the past garden in the mind of Patrick as he held the book up to the light to try to read the Latin names with all the strength in his body.

36
FITCH

Fitch found Valentina near the house, tying up a rose that had been blown over by the wind. She came down the ladder when she saw him as though she had been waiting to talk to him. She seemed agitated.

'What's up?' he said.

'This.' She fanned out her hand towards the garden.

'What do you mean?'

'It's too much. I can't do it.' All around her were the fallen petals of the rose like drops of blood.

'What does Leo say?'

There was a pause. She hadn't talked to him. 'Surely you can only set things in the right direction. You can't stay here for ever.'

'I've been paid to do something I can't do.'

Fitch looked around him. 'What is the aim exactly, anyway?'

'To make it beautiful. All of it.'

'That's going to take years.'

'But it's so important to him.'

'It's only a garden.'

'But it's for her. It's to impress her.' Valentina's forehead ruched up.

Fitch sighed and said patiently, 'She is hardly going to start loving him because he's replanted a few herbaceous borders. Or paid some other people to do it. It's not even her garden!' He felt confident of this. That Miss Vye did not love Leo was as clear as the day.

'I know that but the thing is, he thinks she is.'

'But he's bonkers. She knows that more than anyone. Just do your best. It's all you can do.'

Valentina didn't answer and they could both suddenly hear him playing his harp through the open french windows in the drawing room. Fitch almost laughed but the case of Gabriel Vye was in his mind. He knew that you should be careful when joking about madness. He'd heard whispers that Gabriel Vye was mad. Who was to say that Leo wouldn't do something drastic?

'It's just so terrible that he doesn't seem to realise.'

'What? That she would never fancy him in a million years? Love is blind. He probably does realise, anyway. In his heart of hearts.'

'But he's so depressed. I mean seriously. You never know what people will do when they're in that state.' Gabriel Vye came into Fitch's mind again, a bundle of clothes falling into the sea.

She went back up the ladder and he held it steady at the bottom while she climbed to the height of the first floor windows and he passed her up bits of twine and nails when she needed them. Through the rungs of the ladder he could see the lawn under the big beech tree, stretching out like a stage waiting for the actors to come on.

'Why doesn't he just have a big party on the lawn? Then he could show her the garden as a sort of work in progress thing. She'd probably come to a party.'

He saw Valentina look down on the lawns and at the different areas of the gardens.

'I don't know, Fitch. Would she come? It's just that things are getting past their best now.'

'Exactly. Leave it too late and there'll be no flowers out at all.'

'When could he do it?'

'August? Before the end of the summer holiday. He could invite the whole of Illerwick.'

'It's too late. Everyone will be away.'

'Like who? She won't be. She never goes away.'

'I suppose it would be a chance for me to tell him that it's all going to take a long time to do.'

'I reckon he knows that really.'

They carried on working side by side all morning. In Fitch's opinion, the garden was looking better than it had done for weeks. At last it was colourful and there were fewer weeds. Valentina went to get her radio and they listened to music as they worked and imagined the party with everyone in Illerwick invited. At lunchtime, Leo appeared, dragging an unwieldy assortment of wicker hampers and tartan picnic rugs. He made several trips to the shade of the beech tree on the lawn and they had lunch together. Leo had been making punch. Fitch drank a large glass of it and asked Leo about the party.

Part of him was thinking of impressing Pete and Dave by telling them it was his idea. Part of him was thinking about being at a party with Miss Vye. Leo finished his sandwich before responding but his answer was vague and not really what they had wanted.

He said, 'I've gone off parties.'

Valentina told him her worries about the garden. She forced him to consider the length of time it takes for plants to grow and the importance of planting things at the right time. Fitch had noticed that she had become more knowledgeable recently, although it was not very hard to be more knowledgeable than Leo.

'Even with the idea of the wildflower garden, there is just so much to do and so many structural changes that it will be years before the garden is in any sense finished – if it will ever be,' she was saying.

'I know that. Of course, I know that. It's just . . . it's been something to hold on to, I suppose.' He was pulling up tufts of grass as though he was tearing out his own hair. They waited.

'We would still carry on. Although I can't stay here for ever,' she said.

'I've got my exams next year,' said Fitch, thinking he didn't want to be there for ever either.

Leo looked thoughtful. 'But would she come?' he said. 'That is the question.'

37
LEO

Even in hot weather it was always winter in Beech House. They walked out of the heat and Leo went upstairs, feeling his way through a dazzled blackness to fetch a cardigan. Downstairs, Fitch was practising his scales. Leo caught his reflection in the wardrobe mirror and was shocked. It did not seem so very long ago that it was he who played his scales at that very piano. Now he was alone in the house that he had once shared with his mother and father. He could be nearly halfway through his life. Or more. His mother, a heavy smoker like himself, had died at sixty. You never knew. Halfway through his life with nothing to show for it. He was an only child and yet being alone was always so hard. He looked about the room. Hardly anything had changed in his surroundings; they had just got older and more worn. Like him. He stopped and looked into the cherry tree where blackbirds were gorging themselves as they had done in all the Julys of his life. Lately, death was never far from his mind. Wasn't Hamlet supposed to have been thirty? he thought. I have never felt like this before. I have always been optimistic, thought that things would change, but now I begin to feel that they will not. Have I changed? he wondered. Since I was a boy? I have lived a life of indolence of which I am ashamed. I cannot even do my own garden.

He watched Valentina collecting up her gardening tools and leaning them neatly against the wall of the stable. He thought, what I should be doing is making myself worthy of Melody. I should be writing my instrument book so it will be published and she will take note of me. I should be climbing mountains or doing parachute jumps so she will think I am marvellous and brave. I should be giving piano recitals at the Albert Hall so that she can watch me on television and think that is the man that I will marry and tell everyone we were teenage sweethearts.

A drawing pin in his shoe made his footsteps click as he crossed the chequered hall. He had a fleeting image of himself as a chesspiece, moved by someone who had no idea of the game. He seemed to be his father walking towards himself as a boy doing his piano practice. His father would probably have been wearing Jesus sandals or what he called his desert boots. He thought of his mother, her bare feet dancing on the cool tiles, her anklets tinkling. They did not need much excuse for a party. Perhaps that's why he hated parties now. He stopped with his hand on the door of the room in which Fitch's scales were marching up and down under his sure fingers. Just behind him he felt the past, as if he could turn around and it would still be there: the smoke-filled rooms and incense, the scent of marijuana and patchouli, the couples slinking about on the first floor landings, the long dresses in Indian prints, the faraway insinuation of music. His mother would always ruffle his hair as she passed, or singe him with her cigarette. Other women fussed over him, parading him with his Little Lord Fauntleroy hair. He shuddered.

In summer they spilled like butterflies out on to the lawn and the terraces. Shimmering out across the mown grass in the moonlight where tents were erected that were not marquees but more like Bedouin tents with cushions, and languishing, languorous bodies, smooth and sinewy against the puckered velvet throws. As the years went by, things got brighter and sharper, the music more precise, the singers' voices clearer. Edges were harder.

They must, he realised, have carried on having these weekend house parties when he was sent away to school. While he was shivering in a cold dormitory at the age of eight or nine, sick with longing to be home, they were welcoming their first guests, sipping the first gin-and-tonics of the night. When he came home he always felt he had been missing out on something while he had been away. The routine had always changed; the furniture had moved, they had their meals at different times, they had gone vegan or vegetarian or macrobiotic and all his favourite foods were banned, or they had taken up some new craze or drug. His parents never told him anything. They did not seem to notice him at all. When his father ran off with a Japanese girl his mother pretended that nothing had happened. She carried on smoking. She lived in a cloud of smoke. The parties carried on. More and more people drifted in and out, some of whom lived in the house and some of whom didn't. Another man who he knew only as Danny slipped into his father's shoes. He never spoke to Danny or asked him anything. He wished to appear mature.

His parents' record collection was enormous. He began to investigate it. They encouraged him to like music, arranged for him to have lessons at school on any instrument he chose. Where was his father now? He didn't care. Living in Japan, probably, in a house made of paper.

But the parties, he thought, as Fitch now played *Für Elise*. Could he bear to have one himself? In the later stages he had been quite proud of his mother. She had allowed him so much freedom and told him to invite his friends from school, who thought it all very bohemian. She had received them like a movie star. Melody had come back from university – her first summer holiday – and he and Gabriel had been determined to impress her. He had wanted his friends from school to think that she was his girlfriend. That's how he thought of her. He waited for her to come back. In his memory, he searched the drifts of faces for hers. It had been the last time that anything had ever been any good between them. The final party. He remembered her arriving. She and Gabriel walking arm in arm through the dusk, Gabriel's face full of an expression he often wore but which Leo could never quite decipher. Leo had been smoking, trying to look suave standing on the terrace, his hair greased back. He offered her a glass of champagne. She took it in white-gloved fingers, as graceful as a swan.

In the evening he went to the stable to see Valentina. He lay on the chaise longue and felt himself drowning in black thoughts. He imagined his hair completely flattened, weighted down by black water. Valentina was listening to some music that made him feel sad. It was an old song from his childhood. He wondered why she had it. Its words had never made sense to him and this seemed fitting.

'Have you ever been in love?' he heard himself saying as if someone else were speaking for him.

Valentina did not answer. He lifted up his head to look at her. It felt as though he were wrenching it out of water. She leaned forward and lit a candle on the table. The striking of the match was like a sudden gasp in the silent room. He felt a moment of panic. He had forgotten. He realised now that she would be embarrassed, not knowing that he had already guessed that if she had been in love, it would have been with another woman. She thinks I would not understand, but I would. I am a broad-minded sort of person – I have had to be. For the first time it occurred to him that she might have developed something of a crush on Melody. And yet he felt sure that she could not have known real love. She was too young. He looked across to her eyes but they were hidden in shadow. He noticed that the walls were now laced with strange shapes.

He broke her silence: 'Well, if you ever do, you can think of all the pain it has caused me. Be cautious.'

He sighed and closed his eyes and imagined a party here at Beech House now, so many years later. He thought of how he could make the garden look magical, of how he could line the paths and walk-ways with tiny candles hidden in shells. The music stopped and all he could hear was the sheep crying, mourning the loss of their lambs. From far away there was always the endless lapping of the sea, beyond his hearing and yet always in his ears like the sound of his own breathing, the beat of blood in his veins. He thought of his dear friend Gabriel.

Then her small voice came out of the shadows as clear as a flame. 'I do know about love.'

He opened his eyes and smiled: 'Yes, I expect you do. It is not about age, after all. Juliet was thirteen years old and anyway my love for Melody began when I was younger than you are now.'

'I am twenty-one years old.' She said this rather stiffly, he thought. He waited because it sounded as though there was something more that she had to say. 'I am in love with someone older than me. Someone I can't have. It is typical.'

It was unclear whether she meant that it was typical in general not to be able to have the object of one's affections or whether it was typical that she should not because she was doomed to a life of ill luck. Or whether she often fell for heterosexual women. He thought she could be talking about Melody here.

'So you do know!' he said and leaned up on his

elbows, wishing he could see her properly. Although, as he said this, he wondered whether the love between two women could amount to the kind of grand passion that he called love. Perhaps she had never known love at all, had merely thought she was in love with some girl at horticultural college, or school, a prefect she looked up to, a schoolgirl crush. The girl, now a woman, had probably married and was out of her reach for ever.

'Yes, they're in love with someone else.'

Could this be Melody? Could Valentina be hinting that Melody was in love with him after all but just could not admit it to herself?

'Put that song on again, will you?' he said.

And they remained there in the fantastical, shadowy room, surrounded by sheep, long after the song had finished, neither of them perhaps quite ready to go back to being alone and it seemed to Leo that they were holding something mysterious between them that they were afraid of breaking.

Finally, he got up from where he had been lying, hearing his knees crack, and Valentina got up too. He said, 'It's hard the way our bodies disintegrate, though, isn't it? All of us. Are young women only so beautiful because their beauty is ephemeral?'

Here, he felt he was getting on to ground that they could both share. They were standing in the middle of the room and he had made a move to go but had not.

'The poetical idea of a woman's beauty fading like a flower? The younger woman syndrome? Melody, of course, is older than you.'

'Doesn't seem it though, does she? I feel a hundred years older than her.' He walked to the door. She spoke to his turned back.

'Will you ever give up loving her?'

He smiled at the black paintwork. 'No. I would rather die of love.'

'Do people die of love?'

'Of a broken heart? Yes. I believe they do.'

'Then we are both in danger,' she said and opened the stable door. He took her hand and something made him hold it to his lips. It smelt sweet, of some sort of hand cream like roses. He allowed his lips to touch her warm skin. It was like holding a rose bloom to his face. It was fully dark outside. He wished for the second time that evening to see her face clearly. When he tried to let go of her hand there was a tiny resistance. It was like pulling a plant out of the soil that doesn't quite want to be free. This puzzled him.

38

FITCH

As soon as the concert had finished, it was time to start rehearsing the school play. Miss Vye said that it was going to be *Twelfth Night* and that they would be at an advantage when she was considering who was going to be in it because they had studied it in English. She seemed to catch Fitch's eye. He saw green glass shining under water. He hoped that he would get a speaking part. She said that some of the parts would go to older students who were doing Theatre Studies and that she was still deliberating but that she would put up the notice on the Drama noticeboard before morning break. Fitch turned around and looked at Pete. Suzy was blowing Pete a Marilyn Monroe kiss that she had been perfecting, her Audrey Hepburn phase now over.

Fitch spent the next few hours wondering, if he got a part, which part she would have chosen for him. I will probably be Curio and have two lines, he thought. Or eight words which he could quote already:

Curio: *Will you go hunt, my lord?*
Orsino: *What, Curio?*
Curio: *The hart.*

It will be a punishment for skiving and letting my work slide while she was away. Another reason to hate Boase. At break he and Pete went to the notice-board in the corridor. They didn't rush. They mooched along and made small talk. They both really wanted to be in it. In Fitch's year, it was cool to be in the play because Pete thought it was cool. He could see from the crowd where the notice was. They peered over the smaller heads. Twenty fingers were stabbing at the piece of paper and for a few seconds he did not see his name anywhere but he also noticed that some people had stepped back respectfully when they saw him and this gave him hope. He had never been in the school play before. You never knew. Before he could read his part Suzy said:

'Fitch! Oh my God! You're Feste!'

It said: *Feste (the lady Olivia's fool) – Fitch.*

Suzy was Maria. She was pleased because Miss Vye had added in some extra gentlewomen for Pauline and Lou which meant that it wouldn't be just boys at the rehearsals. Pete, perhaps unsurprisingly for a landlord's son, was the drunkard Uncle Toby, Jimmy Rivers was Andrew Aguecheek and Dave was Fabian. They were all in the sub-plot. The main parts were to be played by sixth-formers. It was all complete typecasting. Pete seemed pleased with his part. He crooked his hand round Jimmy Rivers's neck companionably and

137

started ribbing Dave. Fitch thought, this will change things between us even more.

Fitch was late for the first rehearsal because Boase had kept him behind for laughing. Miss Vye had made everyone put the chairs in a circle. Fitch left his schoolbag by the piano and sat beside Suzy. They had already started reading the play but he knew that he wouldn't be in it for a few scenes. At the end of the first act Miss Vye told them to move the chairs and to choose one of the lines they had just read and walk around saying it in different ways. He chose 'Take away the fool, gentlemen'. Then she got them saying each other's lines in the way that their own characters would say them. Fitch started to enjoy himself. They spread around the room, acknowledging each other as though this was the world of the play. The hall became the court of Orsino, Lady Olivia's house, a deserted shore on the far coast of another country called Illyria. In the space of half an hour, he had shouted, sung, whispered, run helter-skelter round the room and lain still and silently on his back in a kind of meditation. It was at this point that Boase looked in and said something about remembering to shut the high windows. No one moved.

For the last activity, she got them to find a position they thought would be a typical stance adopted by their character. Soon, he saw Orsino lying in an imaginary bower. Viola and Sebastian stood staring at each other so that you could not tell which was which. Olivia stood opposite them in delight, making a triangle. Slowly, the sub-plot got the idea. Suzy sprang to her feet and stood with one hand on her hip wagging her finger at Pete who looked as if he had just let out a belch and was massaging his belly. Jimmy Rivers, as poor Andrew Aguecheek, just seemed to let his whole spine collapse as if he was melting. Fitch looked around in panic. He tried to lie down and put his ear against the ground as if to show he was listening in to everyone's secrets but this didn't seem the real essence of his character. He was the last one. He found that he could not freeze, that to freeze, to be still, did not suit anything about Feste. So he settled for moving and just continued to weave in and out of the statues in a quick-witted kind of a walk.

'Fitch!' Miss Vye said. 'You're supposed to be still. Like a statue. Hurry up and find your pose.'

'I can't, Miss!'

'Well, why not? Come on.'

Fitch was quick in his response. '*Foolery does walk about the orb like the sun, it shines everywhere.*' And for a moment she didn't answer.

Then she said, 'Well done, Fitch. You're really in character. Great poses, everyone. And relax.'

She called them up to the front and Fitch looked around and felt that they were really a proper group. Miss Vye smiled at them and you could tell she was thinking the same thing. Then she said that they had to learn all their lines by the end of two weeks.

'Like fuck,' said Pete quietly.

She clapped her hands once to signal finally that the rehearsal was over and someone seemed to think that it was one of those American things where everyone applauds themselves. Fitch felt embarrassed but Boase was poking his head round the door again so he made a big show of doing it because he knew it was just the sort of thing that would irritate him. He gave a few whoops for good measure.

When they got outside he realised that it had been raining and he hadn't even noticed. He walked with Pete as far as The Crown.

'You're sort of related to Miss Vye aren't you?' he said. He had been wanting to say this for a while but he had never found the right moment.

'Indirectly. Sort of. My dad is her uncle. My mum and dad separated when I was two. Mary's the only mum I've ever known.'

'Oh, right,' Fitch said.

'Don't worry about it,' Pete said. 'I don't remember my real mum.' He patted Fitch on the shoulder adultly. Fitch did not mention his own mother.

Miss Vye passed them on the other side of the street. She didn't have her umbrella and she looked soaking wet with rivulets of rain dripping down her hair and off the end of her chin.

'All right, boys?' she said but she didn't wait for an answer. She seemed to be singing under her breath.

As Fitch climbed the hill to his cottage, the rain petered out. The landscape looked ghostly, the view across the valley cut off by milky fog.

39

MELODY

Melody shivered awake at first light. Her throat felt sore and her limbs watery. She tried to go back to sleep but the faces of Valentina, Leo, Gabriel and Mr Boase all jostled in her mind. She heard the voices of the children from school as if they were all inside her head talking and arguing. She got dressed and shut the bedroom door firmly on them all. From the landing she could see a mist floating above the trees. Waiting for the kettle to boil, she wandered in and out of the gloomy rooms and felt, as usual, that she didn't belong there. Nothing had changed since her parents' time. The books on the study shelves were still the sober, dark blue Oxford University Press editions of this and that, and in the sitting room there were the well-read sets of Dickens, Austen and Trollope which had belonged to her mother, and her grandmother before that. Her father's desk crouched under the study window, everything laid out on it as if he had just left it and gone to church. The same thick curtains, full of the same ancient dust, still shrouded the windows at the back of the house. She sat down heavily on the saggy sofa on which so many ladies of the parish and so many ecclesiastical visitors of the past had perched, sipping cups of tea and being on their best behaviour while she and Gabriel made farting noises from beneath the dining table. The new vicarage that had been chosen by the church when her father had bought this house on his retirement was on the other side of town and seemed a sunny, open sort of house. She did not know if this was fitting for a vicarage or not.

She lay with her tea on the sofa, wrapped in an old Welsh blanket that had rested on the back of it for her whole life and had never, as far as she knew, been washed. She thought, I must have caught a chill when I came home singing in the rain after the rehearsal. The house curled itself around her. She looked around at all the things that her parents had placed in their positions, the worn patches on armchairs and rugs. The way each handle turned and each catch clicked was part of the life they had shared, those two tall, willowy parents of hers, who had their children late in life, and whose gentle temperaments bent this way and that to accommodate each other. And in the garden the story of their marriage continued. She knew which plants each of them had planted and preferred, balancing, complementing each other, working side by side with the wheelbarrow between them filling up with weeds which they tidied so assiduously from between the cracks of the flagstones. They had remained entwined all their lives. Her father's death within a few years of her mother's had been proof of his love.

And, although she wanted to whitewash the walls and take all the furniture to the auction, she found that it was hard because it would be as if she, who had never known what it was to be in love, was destroying the love of her parents. And now there was Gabriel and everything that he had left behind him this last year when there had seemed nowhere else to turn. He had been so frail, a child again, retreating to his old room at the top of the house, with its train track running around the walls and its windowsill that had been turned into an empty station platform where no trains came or went, full of the corpses of flies. His things were still everywhere: his coat was in the hall, his boots in the porch, his little heaps of coins and nails, the contents of his pockets, found unexpectedly on ledges and tables in odd corners.

The darkness of the house was a heavy weight. She fell asleep and dreamed that she painted white emulsion over the tobacco-stained walls and took down the curtains. She emptied the house, heaving everything outside, all the saggy furniture and ornaments and worn pots and pans, and left them in the garden where the river swept them away. She dreamed she closed the front door on emptiness and walked out into the world as she had done when she had gone to Cambridge, the past and her childhood a blur. In her dreams she was like Valentina, who had come to Illerwick to seek adventure. And, it felt, to seek out her. She felt she was on the brink of something, standing on an edge of her own and about to fall.

She opened the front door and went out on wobbly legs, her eyes hurting in the glare. She walked down the empty street and through the graveyard. The church was always left unlocked. She opened the door and stepped into the stone-scented coolness. As she brushed past a flower arrangement, some dry rose petals fell at her feet. She walked the length of the nave and ran her fingers along the smooth backs of the pews. The floor felt uneven. Red and black. Red and black, undulating through the thin soles of her sandals. She passed through the rood screen. She went up to the altar and knelt down in front of the step. She did not believe in God. She saw the coloured shapes of light passing through stained glass that turned her white hands into butterfly wings. She looked up. Outside, the sun came from behind a cloud and found its way into the crevices and corners of the foliage around the ceiling edge and around the broad pillars and shone through the threadbare tapestries high up on the walls. She leaned forward and rested her hands on the rail before the altar. There was a smell of wine. Of bread. Of dying flowers. She pressed her eyes into her knuckles. No sound from outside penetrated. There was a singing inside her ears. She felt faint. She lay down diagonally across the step, resting the side of her head on cold stone. She struggled for breath. She felt a hand on her brow. It felt like her father's. She opened her eyes. There was no one there. She lay for a long time looking back up the nave towards the font that she and Gabriel had been baptised in.

She saw Gabriel standing beside the font. He was undrowned. He smiled at her and she smiled back. She closed her eyes.

She was woken by Mary who came on Saturday mornings to do the flowers. She splashed some of the flower water on her face. They sat still for a while until she felt that she could get up. Her teeth were chattering.

'There's a lot of it about,' Mary said. 'Shall I come back home with you?'

'I'll be all right,' Melody said.

Outside, the sun warmed her face, soothing her. A wind blew across her and flattened the grass. It wasn't far. She went to bed and slept. For two days she was ill but she felt better in her mind than she had done for a long time.

On Monday, after school, she started to clear the house. She took down the curtains and put them in black dustbin liners. She packed everything in boxes and called Mr Worrell, the painter. He came almost immediately as if he had been waiting for her call and covered the floors with dustsheets and set up his ladders. Soon, the house was full of the smell of paint. She went into the garden and cut some sweet peas. She went to the churchyard and put some on her parents' graves. She went to the new cemetery and put some on Gabriel's. She felt better.

40
FITCH

When she was rehearsing the scenes that they weren't in, Miss Vye sent Fitch and the others outside to the playing field to learn their words and practise their scenes. Leo had lent Fitch a guitar and he was using it for his songs he had to sing as Feste. Fitch had given it to Pete to look after and he was strumming under the oak tree in the shade while someone tested him on his lines. Some of the others had started messing about and making grass whistles. Fitch and Suzy moved off to practise their first scene. They had added a few bits of stage business which they were perfecting before they showed it to Miss Vye. Something was happening between them but it was hard to put it into words. After a while they wandered back over to Pete who was leaning with his back against the tree trying out a few riffs. Pauline and Lou had started making daisy chains.

Boase was coming towards them. He was walking across the grass as though grass was a toxic substance. Fitch thought, he is probably coming to say, 'Keep Off the Grass!' but when he eventually reached them it was only to remind them about the Maths exam, which he called the Mathematics Examination, the next day and which they all knew about anyway. At the moment he was focusing his nastiness on Pete. He mainly ignored Fitch now and so Pete was the next obvious target. Pete was even worse than Fitch at Maths.

'You, Peter Flagg, will be sorry if you fail the Mathematics Examination tomorrow.'

Pete shrugged. Boase looked at him silently. Pete was the biggest boy in the year. Behind Boase's small blue eyes, he seemed to be calculating something. Then he stopped calculating. His mouth fell slack. He had seen the girls who were dancing on the bank with their school shirts tucked into their bras.

'What are they doing?' he asked, like some sort of idiot.

Pete looked at the girls moving in unison. The late afternoon sun was glinting in their ponytails. 'What does it look like?' Pete said.

'It looks to me, Peter, as if, like you, they are wasting valuable time.'

He strode over towards them, his pale grey slacks flapping in the wind. They could see him gesticulating and the girls standing with their hands on their hips, outraged by everything he stood for. As he came past again, the girls trailing behind him, he told them to run around the playground picking up litter. There was no litter so they ambled about, pretending to look in the gutters until he was out of sight. A sixth-former appeared and said Suzy and Fitch were needed.

Fitch and Suzy went into the hall and showed Miss Vye what they had been practising. She watched carefully, stopping them every now and then and getting them to repeat some of the lines until she was satisfied. She complimented them on their comic timing. For the next section, Suzy went back outside. This part was harder for Fitch because he was acting with people he didn't really know. Both Olivia and Malvolio were played by sixth-formers and Fitch was afraid of getting out of his depth. He knew this scene was crucial because it marked a turning point for Olivia. The idea was to show that Olivia was the fool and not Feste. Miss Vye said he was to turn the tables on her. The build-up was to the lines:

> *Clown:*   *Good madonna, why mourn'st thou?*
> *Olivia:*   *Good fool, for my brother's death.*
> *Clown:*   *I think his soul is in hell, madonna.*
> *Olivia:*   *I know his soul is in heaven, fool.*
> *Clown:*   *The more fool, madonna, to mourn for*
>   *your brother's soul, being in heaven.*

As he was speaking, Fitch felt a silence creep into the room. It was as if everyone had remembered at exactly the same moment about Gabriel Vye. Everyone knew what had happened at Breakers Point.

'Good!' she said. 'Right, we'll stop there.' It was as if she had not noticed.

Fitch looked at her. Everyone looked at her. She was even paler than usual but she was not sad. She seemed fidgety as if she couldn't wait for them to gather their things and go. He watched her marching along the corridor to her office. By the time he had reached the others in the playing field she was going out of the school gate. She gave her usual little wave.

Pete and the others had been talking about Boase. Pete said that he was a real regular now at The Crown.

'What?' said Suzy. 'I thought he was supposed to be teetotal. I thought he was always lecturing us on the evils of alcohol.'

'I know. That's what my dad says. He hates him. And Mary does.'

'Why?' said Fitch.

'Why what?'

'Why do they hate him?'

'Why do you think?'

'He so loves himself,' Suzy said.

Fitch listened to them going on. He didn't want to waste a minute more of his life thinking about Boase. Now they were making him.

41

JONATHAN

Jonathan is on a train. The train is snaking down the west coast of the island. He is leaning right up against the window-slats so that when there is a curve of track he can see the front part of the train forging ahead like a great orange serpent. Sometimes they are right on the edge of the Indian Ocean, close enough to hear it cascading onto the beach. Sometimes they veer a little inland, crossing the wide mouths of murky rivers and shunting through jungly places and settlements of one kind or another. Everything is familiar and yet it is not. He has travelled right across the world and back to his childhood but he is seeing things with different eyes now. Eyes that had forgotten. Eyes that have been used to the grey tawdriness of London. It is impossible for him to know how much things have changed. There is no one to refer to. No Valentina. He knows the political history, the effects of the war. But there is something hidden which he can't put his finger on.

He had forgotten about the heat. It is inescapable. He has had to relearn how to live in it. How to protect himself from it. Even in the shade of the carriage, he is sweating. A fine layer of reddish-brown dust clings to the sweat on his body. His eyeballs grate in their sockets. He sips from a plastic bottle of warm water and fantasises about getting to Tangalla when he will wade into the sea and be cool. He looks forward to the fall of evening. He sees himself lying naked on a bed in a guesthouse with a fan whirring round above him. In the mean-time he is still crossing off places. He looks at his map. In his head, he is repeating the names of the places they must travel through. The syllables of the words make him remember. He tries to hear where the stresses of the words should fall: Berawela, Bentota, Ambalangoda, Hikkaduwa, Galle, Unawatuna, Weligama, Matara. From Matara, they will get the bus.

Sometimes, there is an unscheduled stop in the middle of nowhere. He sees a chameleon sitting on a post, children running through the trees, a cow, a monk on a bicycle. They go through coconut plan-tations. He looks among the treetops for the toddy tappers. Everything looks like a postcard, like a photograph taken by his parents then. He feels alone here but the carriage is full. No one is speaking English. There is a family opposite him with five children. The children eye him. He smiles at them. They only look and look. Opposite him there is an Australian man he knows, asleep. They met two days ago at the top of Adam's Peak in a cloudy dawn full of enormous moths. His name is Phil and he would describe himself as an experienced traveller. He has listened to Jonathan's stories about when he lived here. He has asked him what it is like to have a twin sister.

From somewhere down the train Jonathan can hear frantic drumming sounds. At the stations there is a scrabble for food, for cool drinks. A man gets on the train singing something familiar which sounds like 'Waddywaddywaddy'. Phil opens one eye. He has got some bananas in his rucksack which they are going to have later. Jonathan cannot stop looking. He looks at the sky, the sea, darker now and spangled; he looks at the crows; he looks at the fishermen sorting out their nets; he looks at the vehicles on the road, the buses, the bicycles and the trishaws. He is remembering a part of his life.

Yesterday he visited the house in Colombo where they used to live. He took a trishaw from Galle Face Green to Colombo 7, where there are wedding cake embassies and the pavements are strewn with frangipani petals. He walked through the garden. He remembered the mango tree, the bougainvillaea. The owners knew he was coming. He had telephoned them beforehand. It is an older couple who live there now. The Da Silvas. All their children are working overseas. One in London and two in New York. They showed him round but it seemed rude to linger. There was a familiar smell of cooking rice. They sat on the verandah and drank lime sodas and he listened politely to the achievements of the children as the Da Silvas showed him lots of photographs of London. He wanted to cry but he could not cry there.

By the time they get to Tangalla, it is late afternoon. They kick off their shoes and walk along the beach. They paddle in the sea. There is no one else around. Phil knows of a good guesthouse. He says he'll go and sort it out if Jonathan minds the rucksacks. Jonathan uses them as a pillow. He lies back. All he can hear is the sea in his ears. His body is relaxing, recovering from the jolting vibrations of the bus and the train. That night they sit on the beach and drink beer. The sky is navy blue and full of stars. The guesthouse owner comes and chats to them. He has owned this guesthouse for five years. There is something hidden which Jonathan can't put his finger on. A small dog interrupts the flow of conversation, howling at the moon.

42

VALENTINA

Valentina was standing in the garden waiting for Leo to come out. She was watching the cherry tree blowing in the wind. A blackbird was riding the breeze in the rocking boughs as if it was in the rigging of a ship. She closed her eyes. The sound of the wind in the leaves in all the trees was like the sound of the sea. And I have never been to the sea on this coast, she thought, even though it is so near. How very unadventurous of me. But I have been rather put off by the thought of people jumping to their deaths in it. She leaned back against the wall and felt the sun on her face and listened to the imaginary waves. When she opened her eyes, Leo was standing beside her, looking anxiously at the terraces.

'Sorry,' she said, 'I was miles away.'

'May I ask where?' he asked gently.

'Sri Lanka,' she said and walked to the top path so they could begin their inspection.

Valentina had now decided that she could cope. After all, she had learned quite a lot over these past few months. She had decided it was time to show

Leo exactly what had been done and what needed to be done in the future when it was the right season or when the right person could be found for the job. The roses, now fading a little, she had pruned in the spring. She had tied up the climbers and cleared away the weeds that were choking the rose beds. There was no question of uprooting any of them. She thought of them as very old, aristocratic people who should be left to their own devices. Leo was wandering down an avenue of Gloire de Dijon. She watched him stop and lift a heavy-headed bloom to his nose and smell it wistfully. She knew all the names now and had attached some discreet labels so Leo wouldn't forget. The centrepiece of the rose garden was a wooden gazebo which had collapsed under the weight of a rose called Kiftsgate; she was still looking for a local carpenter who would be able to come and restore it. In the autumn some new specimens could be introduced. The flagstones that divided the beds had stood the test of time. Now she had planted thyme between them. Leo had told her that, hundreds of years ago, they had been the slates on the church roof, but he was not sure how they came to Beech House.

'Stolen?' she suggested.

She led the way along the first of the three levels of terraces. Tucked under her arm were her notes from the visits to Patrick and the jigsaw drawings she had made of how the beds should look. She had still not found the right moment to tell Leo that Patrick was still alive. She felt a panic that he might die before she said anything. The terraces were very sheltered, which meant that unusual and tender plants could be grown against the brick walls. Some things had survived, like a dark purple buddleia and a bottle-brush tree, and they were looking healthier because she had dug over the soil and fertilised it with chicken manure. She listed varieties of geranium, campanula, phlox and oriental poppy that would all be planted in the autumn to create a summer border of blue, white and pink, romantic colours, which Leo had said he thought Melody would like. When these plants stopped flowering there would be others that would take their place. She showed Leo some pictures she was carrying, although she could see that it was hard to imagine it now, just looking at the bare patches of earth. As a temporary measure, she had put in flowers she had grown from seed and there were white drifts of cosmos and larkspur and some love-in-a-mist, and she and Fitch had trimmed the box hedges. Leo was charmed by these things. On the other side, the plan was for hot colours – for reds and yellows, for crocosmia, rudbeckia, red hot pokers and day lilies – but the clearing process was still in operation. Glyn had brought another man to help him but progress was slow. No more planting could take place for a few months.

They went into the orangery. It was empty, except for the wrought iron benches and some heaps of cushions and a wicker chair Leo had brought in. The red, tiled floor was cracked but they agreed it was strangely beautiful as it was. She had researched the exact ferns that could be grown and had thought that to grow what in Sri Lanka they had called the

Queen of the Night and jasmines and any other very scented plants would be just what Leo would need to help him compose his songs or write whatever he wrote in his dark green notebook. The main things that the orangery needed were the citrus trees and Leo had ordered them from a nursery, which would be sending them any day. They sat and looked across at the cypresses and the yew hedges at the bottom of the terraces.

'And the topiary animals?' said Leo.

'Pick your animal.'

'Ah, lions, I think.'

She smiled at him, and said, 'Are you sure you don't want peacocks?'

'Oh, I am having real peacocks. The chicks are arriving on Wednesday. They will be my responsibility.'

'Well, it's your garden,' she said.

'And hers,' he reminded her, awkwardly.

They looked through the notes and books for a while and they discussed the clearing process, the plans for the wildflower meadow, the water garden in the wood, the restoration of the summerhouse and the tennis courts and the creation of the maze. They had already filled the pond with water lilies the previous week.

'It has taken so much time to clear everything and there's still so much to do,' she was saying, wondering if she could ever bear to leave and knowing that if Leo did not love her she could not stay. He interrupted her. It was as if the garden was now the last thing on his mind.

'I think, by the way, that the party is a good idea. Melody will be the guest of honour.'

He leapt up, full of jumbled ideas. He talked of candles in shells lighting the paths. Of homemade punch served in antique glasses. She calmed him. She said that the party could take place in the orangery. They could have a marquee on the lower lawns for dancing. He looked grateful to her for making it so simple. He made her laugh.

'For this party,' he said, 'money will be no object. I will use the money that I had put aside for the roof. I will invite everyone in the town.'

'And when will the great occasion take place?'

'August 14th,' he said, immediately. 'My birthday.'

'And who are you going to get to help you do all the invitations?'

'You will be suspended from gardening duties to help me compose them. We will do them on the computer today. Fitch will deliver them.'

They remained still. Valentina was remembering the way he had kissed her hand in the stable doorway. She wanted to touch him, to place her cheek against the warm skin on his neck.

'You'd better come up to the house,' he said and she followed him into the icy hall.

43
FITCH

The latest gossip at school was that Pete had caused an argument between Miss Vye and Mr Boase. They had been in the middle of a rehearsal. Viola had just done her '*I left no ring with her*' speech and Feste, Sir Toby and Sir Andrew were all needed for the scene when Maria comes and tells them they are doing too much caterwauling. Fitch had been so nervous about the fact that he had to sing his first song, '*O mistress mine, where are you roaming?*' that he had not even noticed that Pete was missing. It was Suzy who had remembered that he was in detention every night that week for getting 16 per cent in his Maths exam.

'What?' said Miss Vye. 'Does the fact that he is one of the main parts in the school play mean nothing to anyone?'

There had been a shifty silence during which she seemed to expect that someone would tear off down the corridor and go and tell Boase that he had made a big mistake and could he hand over Pete immediately so they could get on with their rehearsal, which was obviously far more important than his silly little detention. Obviously, no one had moved.

'Fine! I'll have to go myself!' She had slammed her script down on the piano and gone stalking out of the hall.

'Uh-oh,' Jimmy had said, nervously, but you could see that there were wild birds of laughter and jubilation in his soul at the thought of Boase being in the shit.

Five minutes later, she had appeared with Pete in tow and the rehearsal had continued as though nothing had happened. The only thing that had been different was that Boase had not come and reminded them about closing the windows. In the break, Pete said that Miss Vye had burst into Boase's classroom and given him what for. She had told him that he had no business dishing out detentions to boys who were giving their all in the school play five nights a week. And there had been another thing. Boase had told him that because he had got such a low mark he would have to repeat the year. 'What, like go back a whole year of your life to be with all the morons in the year below?' Suzy whispered. Pete said yes it would have done, but Miss Vye had put a stop to it. She had said 'Nonsense!' And when they were going up the corridor afterwards, she had said, 'I am the headmistress, Pete, and what I say goes. You are not repeating the year. You are far too good at English for that.' Pete had quoted her words verbatim. He said she was steaming. He said he had to run to keep up with her.

'Obviously,' Dave said, 'he's getting far too big for his Hush Puppies.'

'Yeah!' said Jimmy.

But it turned out that there was something that Pete had not told everyone. He showed Fitch and Suzy when they got back to his place. It was not a very warm evening and it was threatening rain so they went and chilled, literally, in the beer garden. Pete lifted his fringe and showed them a mark above his left eye. They waited.

'Board rubber,' he said. 'Poor reflexes. And he called me a lump of lard.'

Fitch was not really surprised. Boase had seemed to be building up to something all week.

'Bastard,' said Suzy, protectively. Fitch noticed that the more rehearsals they had, the more interested she seemed in Pete. Her eyes flicked back at him across the table to see what he thought of this.

Mary was hanging out washing in the yard and when she saw that they were back from the rehearsal she put down her basket. She was younger than most people's mums, even though Jack Flagg was quite old, and she liked to be in with Pete's friends. Fitch noticed that she was pregnant, which was something Pete had not mentioned.

'All right, gang?' she said, 'How's the play going?'

They all said fine. Fitch felt embarrassed. He stared down at her blue nail-varnished toes sticking out of her sandals.

Suzy said, 'When's it due?'

Fitch was thinking about Boase. He was remembering the fear of him he had felt when Miss Vye had not been there to keep him in check. He was thinking of the time when he had caught the board rubber in mid-air. Of the figure he had seen slumped over Miss Vye's desk. He wanted to tell them. He wanted to be able to tell them why he stopped coming to school and the way he felt now that he had something on Boase which felt like ammunition that could be used against him if the occasion arose.

Mary had seen the mark.

'What have you done to your head, Pete?' she said. She reached out a hand and smoothed away Pete's hair.

He flicked her hand off. 'Nothing,' he said. Fitch and Suzy became suddenly very interested in a couple of magpies at the bottom of the garden.

'You haven't been in a fight, have you?'

'No.'

She looked at their faces in turn before going back to the yard. Fitch watched her go inside to the kitchen where the dark figure of Jack Flagg could be seen stacking glasses.

When she'd gone, Suzy said: 'You should tell her, you know.'

'Leave it,' said Pete.

And then Fitch found that it was more to lighten the mood that he told them about what had happened. And it was at this moment, he thought later, that he had discovered his gift for making even the most painful things seem hilarious. When he finished the story, Pete laughed more than Fitch had ever seen him laugh before.

Suzy laughed a bit but then she said, 'That is disgusting. Does that mean you actually saw his . . . you know what?' She wiggled her little finger.

'I tried not to look,' he said.

'I can't believe you called him a wanker to his face,' said Pete.

He walked part of the way home with Suzy. Suzy insisted on peering in at the windows of the pub but Boase was nowhere to be seen. They ran through their lines as they went along.

'We've got to be word perfect by tomorrow,' Suzy said.

'We are.'

She looked very pretty, standing there at the end of her road. There was a moment, as there was often now, when it seemed like she was offering him something without words but he let it pass, as he usually did. She smiled but there was a hard, disappointed look in her eyes. She turned to walk up to her bungalow. He watched her to see if she would turn round and she didn't. When he walked past Miss Vye's house all the shutters were closed but there were thin slivers of light glowing behind them. He wondered what it was like inside.

The next day, Pete had the hint of a black eye. He said he'd told Mary and his father about the detention and the threat of going down a year but not about the board rubber.

'What about the shiner?'

'I said you threw a tennis ball and it hit me in the eye.'

'Thanks a lot. Did she believe you?'

'Yes. She told me I'd better do more revision for Maths next time.'

When he got home from school, Fitch found his father and Valentina in the garden talking about slug control. He noticed how both his father and the dogs had taken an immediate liking to Valentina. She was like that; wherever she went she was accepted for who she was. She was good at asking questions but no one ever seemed to ask her any questions. He wanted to ask her quite a few things: for example, why had she left the real world to come to a place like Illerwick? Normally people of her age were going the other way. Another question he wanted to ask was about Miss Vye. What was she like when the two of them were alone together, when she wasn't being a headmistress? When she was Melody.

Valentina had a proposition for him. If he would distribute all the invitations by next Saturday, Leo would give him a week off and a bonus and he would get to bring as many of his friends to the party as he wanted. He looked at the carrier bag full of invitation cards.

'How many people is he inviting?'

'Lots,' she said, passing over the bag.

He left them to their vegetable talk and went and practised his songs in his bedroom while they were well out of earshot. His father seemed cheered by Valentina's company. He heard him whistling as he took off his boots in the hall. He seemed to find the whole idea of the party very amusing, especially the idea that he would be attending it.

'Dressed up like a dog's dinner?' said Fitch.

44
FITCH

Fitch had two invitations left. He crumpled up the carrier bag and threw it in the dustbin by the bus shelter. Then he sat on the edge of the war memorial and looked at the two envelopes. He put one in the inside pocket of his blazer and one in the badge pocket outside. He went to the river and looked over the bridge with his back to Miss Vye's house. A shoal of minnows flickered in the sun. He took the envelope from the outside pocket and held it above them. He imagined dropping it into the green water and watching the minnows devouring it like piranhas. A car went past behind his back. He knew she was in; the shutters and the windows had been wide open all day. He thought, I should just drop hers through the letterbox now. He felt the corners digging into his chest through his shirt. One in the water, one in the letterbox, he thought.

He went towards the house. He thought he could hear her singing. He remembered the sirens in *The Odyssey*, which he had read last year. He imagined she was one. He heard a van draw up behind him.

He stepped aside and watched Mr Worrell, the painter, climb out and go up to the little gate.

'All right, Fitch?' he said, raising his spattered eyebrows.

Fitch did not reply. He got on his bike and rode up to the castle. He left his bike in the wood and lay on the grass. His stomach was fluttering and his pulse seemed to be getting faster instead of slower as he took deep breaths of humid air. Behind him, upside down, he saw the last remaining tower of the castle. He imagined it toppling over him and burying him in rubble. He closed his eyes and thought about kissing Suzy but Miss Vye's face kept getting in the way. The sun beat hotly down onto his body. He felt himself becoming part of the earth. He opened his eyes and sat up. He tossed one of the invitations into the gorse and listened to the cropping of sheep higher up the slope, to the cries of buzzards wheeling above him. Five minutes later, he went and retrieved it.

In Illerwick, the sun was turning everything into gold. The sky was full of house martins catching flies. Mr Worrell's van had gone. Her windows were still open. He put his hand on the gate. He wanted to open it without making the least sound. He looked up at the windows. She was standing on a chair doing something inside that he could not see. She saw him and laughed. He heard her footsteps thudding down the stairs.

'Fitch!' she said as she opened the door. 'Come and see this.'

He followed her in. There were mounds of invisible things under dustsheets.

'Ignore those,' she said.

She opened the door of the first room. It felt cool. The walls had been painted white but the late sun had turned them faintly pink, as though they were blushing. The smell of new paint rushed into his nostrils and caused a tiny, sharp feeling in his forehead. She led him through the empty rooms, her feet bare, her hair in an untidy topknot. He walked behind her, his eyes level with the nape of her neck. They stood in the largest room with boxes all around.

'What do you think?' she said.

The walls had begun to infect his mind with their blankness. He said, 'Nice.'

She sat down on the edge of a box. Anyone else would have crushed it with their weight. 'Are you all right?' she said. 'How are your piano lessons going?'

'OK,' he said. He held out the envelope and watched her press her lips together when she recognised Leo's handwriting. She put it in the back pocket of her jeans. He didn't leave. She moved towards him. She put her hands on his shoulders and looked into his face. He wanted to lean against her. He felt himself shaking.

'Is something wrong, Fitch?'

'I'm fine,' he said.

'It's not the play, is it? I'm glad I cast you. At first, I thought you might be unreliable. But I was wrong.'

'No,' he said, 'it's not the play.'

There was a pause. He breathed in the smell of her perfume.

'I'd best be going,' he said. He thought that if she took her arms away, he would crash to the ground.

'Yes. OK.' She led him to the door. His feet felt strange and heavy as if his shoes were full of water.

She watched him go down the path.

'See you tomorrow,' she called as if she was afraid she would not.

He wheeled his bike away, looking back and smiling wildly until he reached the corner. Then he leaned the bike against the post office wall and pretended to read the notices in the window until he felt normal.

Cycling past The Crown, he saw Suzy. 'What are you doing?' he said.

'Waiting for Pete.'

He heard a door slam and Pete came out. Neither of them was wearing their school uniform.

'All right?' said Pete.

He wanted to ask where they were going but something stopped him. Pete sat on the wall and Suzy sat next to him.

'We're going to the weir,' Suzy said, not moving.

'What're you up to?'

'Delivering the invitations for the party. Haven't they got theirs?' Fitch nodded his head in the direction of the pub kitchen. Pete shrugged. He didn't seem that interested. Fitch felt inside his pocket for Boase's invitation. He held it up so they could read the name on it.

'One left,' he said.

'Why is he invited?'

'Everyone is.'

'Shouldn't think he'll bother going, anyway.'

Suzy had taken the envelope from him. 'Let's have a look,' she said. She slid the card out of the envelope and read it. Then she quickly put it behind her back. Pete touched his arm.

'What?' Fitch said.

'Don't look now.'

Fitch looked. He moved and sat next to Suzy on the wall. Boase was walking past on the other pavement. He was staring at the hills at the end of the street as if he planned to hike up them before dusk fell. He tripped slightly on an uneven paving slab and looked back at it accusingly. The three of them in a line watched him. They did not dare to laugh until he had reached the mulberry tree.

'I've got an idea,' Suzy said.

'What?'

'These are done on the computer, aren't they?'

Fitch nodded.

'Can I borrow this?'

He shrugged. He didn't care what happened to it.

'What are you going to do?'

'Wait and see!'

Pete was shuffling about. He seemed bored, anxious to get going while there was still light left.

'Are you coming?'

Fitch shook his head. He watched them go down the street. Before they reached the corner, he turned away. By the time he got home, the light was disappearing. When he had put his bike away, his father was coming in from the garden. He tucked his arm through Fitch's and whistled over his shoulder to the dogs. They climbed the steps to the door together like an old married couple. The dogs were their children. Fitch felt like bawling his eyes out but he just turned on the TV and hugged the dogs on the sofa.

45
MELODY

Melody went back inside and stood in the empty sitting room. She took the envelope from her pocket and opened it with a heavy heart. It said:

> *Leo Spring requests the pleasure of the company of Miss Melody Vye at a Party, to be held at Beech House, Illerwick, on Saturday, August 14th, at 7.00 p.m., to celebrate his birthday and the work in progress in the gardens.*
> *Evening Dress.* RSVP

She put it face down on the windowsill and went back to unpacking boxes. She gathered up a dust-sheet and threw it out into the garden. Inside one of the boxes that had been beneath it was Gabriel's duffel bag. Still she had not opened it. She could not seem to put her hand inside. She did it up again, put it back in the box and stuffed the box into the cupboard under the stairs. Then she went into the garden to get the dustsheet in case it rained overnight. She sat holding it on the bench, feeling jumpy. A quick gust of wind rippled through the hedge as though someone had brushed past it. She shivered and rocked herself in the sudden cold. A car went past with music inside it. She thought of Leo standing on the terrace, like a lonely sentinel, waiting to receive her, holding out his arm for her to take and be led inside. She thought of Valentina, her face with moonlight on it, like a dusting of pollen on a butterfly's wings. She wondered if Valentina was avoiding her.

The next day, the sky was so blue that she made an announcement that the play would be performed outside.

'What if it rains?' said Dave.

'We will have a contingency plan,' she said and to herself she added, I know it will not rain.

She walked round the playing field until she found a patch of ground in the middle of what used to be an orchard. She told Mr Boase that he was to arrange for some blocks that were kept under the stage in the hall to be carried out. She thought that they could tie lengths of material to the trees to be like the wings. Mr Boase went to see the caretaker straight away, even though it was morning break. He left his coffee untouched on the table in the staffroom. The disagreement about Pete had never been mentioned.

At the rehearsal she sat on a chair amongst the apple trees and made them repeat their lines if she could not hear them. It was still hot, even at five o'clock, and she had to wear her straw hat so that she didn't burn. Fitch seemed better. When he sang, people held their breath. There had been a shift, a transformation, in the last week and the children had seemed to become their characters, even without their costumes. Their voices, their movements seemed to belong to the people that Shakespeare had imagined. When they stumbled over their words, or did not perfectly understand them, it did not matter. She believed in the essence of them. They were taking the play very seriously and she felt touched by this, because it was as though they had decided that because of what had happened to Gabriel they did not want to let her down. She wondered what Valentina would think of the play. Her stomach flipped over at the thought of her being there, watching the performance that she had brought into being. There were only a few days to go.

But when the rehearsal had finished and she went home, she found Valentina waiting outside her house. She was standing firmly on the concrete path as if she had been there for hours.

'I was just passing,' she said, dully. 'Are you coming to his party?' She did not try to disguise that Leo had sent her. Her eyes stayed glued to the nasturtiums tumbling over the edges of the path.

'To tell you the truth,' Melody lied, 'I don't know.'

Valentina lifted her eyes to look at her for the first time. They were almost turquoise. Melody saw herself walking across a dance floor inside a hot marquee and Valentina weaving in front of her through the knots of limbs, leading her out into a plush darkness of whispering leaves. She knew she would go to the party, whatever it would do to Leo.

'Well, when you do know, can you let him know?

RSVP,' Valentina said crisply and turned to go without saying goodbye.

The sight of Valentina's turning shoulders panicked her.

'Have you been doing any more writing?' she said too quickly.

'Some.'

'Meet me after school, tomorrow. The rehearsal finishes at six. I can show you that walk we were going to go on last time and you can tell me more about your writing. Then I can tell you what I have decided about the party.'

'OK.' Valentina's voice sounded like a robot's. She snatched at a handful of grass seeds from the bank as she walked away. Melody thought, she will not come.

She went inside and dragged some furniture around. Her footsteps echoed on the boards where she had taken up the old carpet. She was tired. She went upstairs and lay guiltily on her bed.

'Well, what am I supposed to do?' she said aloud, as though Gabriel was sitting in the window seat.

In the stable, Valentina was smoking a cigarette from a packet Leo had left on the table. She sucked the smoke deep inside her lungs. She watched the milky threads curling endlessly above her, ravelling and unravelling their silky knots. On her knee was her open journal in which she had written two headings: Reasons for Leaving. Reasons for Staying.

46

MR BOASE

An envelope was there when he came home in the almost-darkness. It was glaring white against the dark bristles of the doormat. He bent forward, losing his balance slightly, and scrabbled for its edges with his dry fingers. He took it into the lounge and slumped on the sofa, savouring the delicate fantasy that the dark curvaceous handwriting was hers, knowing that it was not. He remembered the valentine he had sent her. The remains of the rose pink tissue paper that he had smuggled from the Art room lay gathering dust on the shelf above the television. Every time they rustled in a draught, he felt ashamed. He opened the envelope and drew out the square of card with shaking fingers. The black printed letters jumped about. Slowly, he absorbed the words:

Leo Spring requests the pleasure of the company of Mr Derek Boase at a Party, to be held at Beech House, Illerwick, on Saturday, August 14th, at 8.00pm, to celebrate his birthday and the work in progress in the gardens.
Fancy Dress.   *RSVP*

'Whatever next?' he said to the blank face of the television and went, with a beating heart, into the kitchen to get his whisky and to force down a tin of vegetable soup.

It was a long time since he had been invited to a party. Party invitations made him think of when he was a child after the war. A picture came to him, perhaps it was a photograph he'd once seen, of himself in his first bow tie, with wetted-down hair and a grim smile. Parties then meant Pass-the-Parcel, Musical Chairs and Blind Man's Buff. There had not been many others since those days. Or any that he cared to remember.

But why would Leo Spring, a man of whom he strongly disapproved, and whose hair he found distinctly alarming, invite him to a party? No one invites me to parties, he thought; I am a well-known killjoy. But, although he disapproved of Leo Spring, he was in awe of him. He was in awe of his house, with its red, barley-sugar chimneys that he had seen from the lane; he was in awe of its high garden walls, which he had seen from the beech woods. But more than this, he was in awe of the fact that Melody was one of those privileged to go beyond the high walls and had, indeed, gone there as a girl. Leo Spring was her friend. He felt as though something inside him might burst.

In the days since he had angered her over Peter Flagg, he had wanted to die. Again and again in his mind, he had seen the look she cast him from the doorway when she took the boy away. He could only think of the word withering. It was a withering look.

He had sat with his head in his hands for a long time. He had crept away from the school, feeling like an outcast, leaving the sounds of voices in the hall far behind him. That night, he could not face the red darkness of the pubs and had drowned his sorrows at home. He could not go to The Crown.

He did not resent her for making him look a fool, he only wanted not to look a fool any more, for her to admire him because he had done the right thing, not the wrong thing. Today, he had gone against the grain and helped her with the school play. Normally, he steered well clear of it; he would stay in his classroom writing reports and devoting the last days of term to lectures about lost property and untidy classrooms. But today, today, he had himself helped Reg Thomas to carry out the staging into the playing field. He had not said that the hot weather was sure to break and they would all be drowned. He had said that if there was anything, anything at all, that needed doing, behind the scenes of course, then he was the man to do it.

He needn't have more than the odd glass of wine at the party. He might not even touch a drop. He could take a little flask and put it in his pocket for emergencies. He would control himself, pace himself, throughout the evening. What to wear? Evening dress, he thought anxiously, rummaging mentally through the ancient apparel in his wardrobe. He picked up the invitation again. Fancy dress! His heart sank at the unusual instruction. He had never been to a fancy dress party before – or perhaps he had; he remembered faintly that his mother had dressed him as an acorn or an elf or something of that nature, once, long ago, and he had gone to a village hall and mingled with pirates and ghosts and been afraid because he couldn't recognise anyone. He could never go if it was fancy dress. Unless it was a disguise. Unless he wore something that would enable him to merge with the crowd.

But in the morning his head ached. He glanced at the invitation lying in a pool of cold soup. He saw his old face in the hall mirror. He decided that he would not go.

47

VALENTINA

Melody and Valentina were on the top of Bryn Mawr, sitting on the grass with their backs against a rock. It had been the hottest day of the year and it was still hot. Everything was shimmery, the faraway mountains were pale blue shadows and the sea was invisible. Melody pointed out the wobbling outline of the castle, buried in green, on an opposite hill. All the way up the steep path, she had seemed exhilarated. She had carried the picnic hamper as if it had been no weight at all, and yet she was breathless, her white skin flushed and all her freckles melted away. Valentina felt exhausted. She had been planting up the fruit trees in the orangery all afternoon and the air had been stifling. Her back and shoulders ached from lifting terracotta pots that were too heavy for her.

Now Melody was pouring yellow wine into fluted glasses. Valentina took her glass and rolled it tentatively to and fro against her cheek. All she wanted was a long drink of water. She watched Melody arranging some cheese and fruit on little plates as if she were setting up a still life. All the time she was talking. She was talking about the play, about the illusion of the sea that they would create with whispers, about Mr Boase offering to do front-of-house, about how she had kept the wine and cheese in the fridge in the school kitchen. Then she stopped talking as if she had run out of time. She closed her eyes and leaned back. Valentina watched her flickering eyelids, the way her pulse beat in her neck. The blush in her face was subsiding and the freckles reappearing. Valentina did not begrudge her this moment of happiness. If she was not thinking of Gabriel, then that was surely a blessing.

'I saw him,' she said, suddenly, without opening her eyes.

'You can't have done. Leo's in London today, seeing about decorations for the party.'

'No. I meant Gabriel. But not today, a while ago. I saw him in the church.'

Valentina did not reply. She was the sort of person who did not believe in ghosts. She waited.

'He just smiled and I felt better.'

They looked at the evening laid out before them. Valentina found she wanted to tell Melody things. She wanted to tell her that she missed Jonathan and that he was on the other side of the world in the middle of the night and she had argued with him because he wanted to go to Sri Lanka on his own. She wanted to ask what it was like if you were not a twin. She recognised that these were things that you could not say to someone whose brother had gone mad and jumped off a cliff.

Melody was offering her more wine and refilling her own glass. Valentina looked at the gradually warming glass in her hand and realised she had not taken one sip. In the distance, she thought she heard a seagull crying.

'*I must down to the seas again*,' she said without thinking.

'*To the lonely sea and the sky*? I'll take you.'

'No, I . . . I'm sorry.' She had been tactless.

'I'll take you in my car.'

'I'm sorry. I'm sure you don't really want to go.'

'Don't worry.' She put her hand on Valentina's. It felt like hot stone. With her other hand Melody refilled her own glass again.

'Your story,' she said, 'was beautiful. Have you written any more?'

Valentina removed her hand. 'I think I must have writer's block.'

'That's a pity because you are a writer, not a gardener, aren't you. I expect Leo keeps you very busy. It must be difficult.'

'Well, the party . . . He's gone to a lot of trouble.'

For you, Valentina thought. He's gone to a lot of trouble for you. And he wants to know if you are coming or not.

Melody took a sliver of peach.

'I shouldn't go, really.'

'But?'

'Obviously, I shouldn't go. Because of what happened at New Year. Because he will get the wrong idea and only be hurt later. More to the point, you shouldn't think I should go, if you have his interests at heart.'

'How do you know that I think you should go?'

'Well, do you?'

'Yes.'

'Well, if you think I should, I will.'

'Promise?'

'If there are lots of other people there, I won't have to talk to him much. I can talk to you if I get bored. So, yes, I promise I will go.' She started to laugh but Valentina talked over her laughter and drowned it out.

'You must talk to him.'

Valentina thought, now he will be able to go on. Now I will not have to watch his heart breaking and I will be able to leave him on a good note. It does not matter if I break my heart. I am younger and stronger and I have more years in which to put it back together.

'All right. If you say so. As long as I can talk to you, too.'

Valentina looked at Melody's haughty face beneath her sun-reddened hair and was so relieved she wanted to hug her. She leaned across the picnic rug and put her arms around her.

'Thank you for saying you will come. I don't know what he'd do if you said no.'

When she let go, Melody seemed to fall against her.

'Sorry,' she murmured, heaving herself upright again against the rock. She left her hand on Valentina's arm as though she had forgotten that it belonged to her.

Valentina thought they should be going. The sun would set soon.

'I could stay here for ever,' said Melody.

Valentina did not move. The arm was like a dead arm that didn't belong to either of them. They sat still on the rug and watched darkness beginning to come down.

Melody interrupted it. She held out both her arms as if she wanted Valentina to fall inside them. She said, 'I love you.'

Valentina stood up and spilled her glass of wine on the rug. She saw Melody's arms fall down. She said, 'I'd better go.'

She skidded down the path and caused the sheep to stampede. She trampled through the bracken and made the crows go mad in the trees. She crashed into the gate at the bottom of the field and scattered rabbits. Even when she reached the main street in Illerwick she kept running and made all the dogs bark.

When she got to the house, there was no sign of Leo. She wandered alone in the dark garden and felt afraid. Even though it was dark, she heard a bird still singing. She had to leave. She would leave before the party if she had to. She lay fully dressed on her bed in the stable letting her ears catch her tears until she heard his feet on the gravel path like feet on a lonely shore on the other side of the world. She wanted to go to him, to unbolt the door and fly out into the darkness and fall into his arms.

48
FITCH

It was the day of the school play and even by mid-morning it was hotter than ever. The summer holidays would start tomorrow. In school, lessons had fallen by the wayside. In all the classrooms half-hearted games of Hangman were going on. Teachers were resting at their desks letting everyone mess about, but anyone who was anyone was helping with the last-minute preparations for the play. Fitch and some other boys were carrying stacks of chairs to be set out on the grass when Fitch saw Boase weaving towards him between the apple trees. He put down the chairs and wiped his face with the edge of his tie. Boase told him to tuck in his shirt. He did not really look at him. Now, he always kept his eyes on some personal horizon when addressing Fitch. He told him that Miss Vye wanted to see him in her office. He added 'at the double' which was an expression both of them knew that she would never have used. Fitch walked slowly across the playground, racking his brains to think what it could be about. He stopped and turned, halfway across, almost thinking of going back to Boase and demanding to know what she had said to him, except that there would be no point because she would never have told him, anyway. He looked back at the stooped figure under the trees, lining up the chairs, counting with a pointing finger the number in each row, and felt almost sorry for him. It was so obvious why he was pretending that he cared about the play all of a sudden.

The door of Miss Vye's office was wide open. She was holding the telephone receiver to her ear, as if she was about to make a call but when she saw him she put it down. Fitch thought, is it Dad? He gripped the edge of the wide desk. The window was open and some girls went past, giggling. Miss Vye started opening the drawers, looking for something. She seemed flustered. This room was supposed to be her office but she never used it. She left her things in her classroom and that was where she was normally to be found.

'Why are there never any envelopes?' she said.

'There's a pile on the shelf above your head.'

'Oh.' She reached up and stuffed a handwritten note into an envelope. Fitch read, upside down, the name she was writing on the outside. He breathed again; it was not his father.

'I want you to take this to Valentina. To Beech House.'

'Now?' He looked at her steadily.

'Yes. It won't take you very long. Go and find her, wherever she's working. You'll be back by lunchtime.' She was blushing. With her pale skin, it was hard to hide.

'OK.' He noticed she had shadows under her eyes.

He put it inside his shirt pocket. He was beginning to feel like Postman Pat.

When he went past her window, he heard a tapping sound and saw that she was mouthing the words 'Thank you'. He shrugged. Little did she know that for her he would go to outer space and be back by lunchtime.

Boase was coming towards him. Fitch speeded up slightly so that he would be strolling through the school gates right in front of him.

'And where do you think you're going?' Boase said predictably.

Fitch gave him a little wave. 'Venus,' he said and then kicked himself for not saying Uranus.

The town was quite busy. A few people gave his school uniform a second look but no one said anything. The church clock chimed twelve. He bought an apple in the greengrocer's. He was so hot by the time he got to the fields, he took off his shirt and tied it round his waist but it was cooler in the beech wood. Pigeons plashed above him in the high green waves of the trees. He thought he'd better put his shirt back on and then he panicked and thought the letter might have fallen out. It was still there. From then on, he held it in his hand, carefully, by the edges, so that it didn't get sweaty. He didn't feel like rushing. There was nothing to get back for. They wouldn't have to get changed for the play until five or six.

In the very heart of the wood, he was dreaming and he dropped the letter. The ground was hard and dry because of the hot weather so it was unfortunate that it found its way into a muddy patch. He picked it up and dusted it off but there was still a smudge of mud on one corner which he tried to clean off with a dock leaf. It was only here, and at this moment, in the dark secrecy of the wood that he decided to read it. He had known all along that she hadn't licked down the envelope. He had dismissed the idea several times before now when he was out in the open. He told himself he was checking that no mud had got inside. Carefully, he took out the single sheet, hardly daring to unfold it as he read the neatly written words with half an eye.

Fitch carefully put the letter back inside the envelope and put it back in his pocket before allowing his shock to register. He took it out of his pocket and checked that it was definitely Valentina's name on the outside. He sat down on a tree stump.

'Fucking hell.'

The trees deadened his words. They might as well have been the droning of a gnat.

He did not know how he arrived at Beech House. In the distance, he saw Valentina, Leo and a man who seemed to be demonstrating acrobatics on the lower lawns. He could not bring himself to go up to them. He felt that the letter was burning him. He went to the stable, opened the top part of the door and dropped it over as if he was throwing it off the edge of a cliff. It lay on the mat in a hot band of sun.

He bunked off school for the rest of the day. At home he told his father that they had been given time off for good behaviour and helped him to pick broad beans and dig up the potatoes to try to get rid of the lump in his throat. He lay under the apple tree in the shade with his back to his father working. He thought, I have been a fool.

49

LEO

Early evening. In the cool of his bedroom, Leo was trying on shirts to wear to the play. Valentina had gone on ahead. She had said something about visiting someone but he had hardly listened. He said he would see her there. Finally, he selected white cotton and the lightest-weight cream linen jacket he could find. He went over to the basin and ran damp fingers through his hair, averting his eyes from the white strands. It was still early. He descended the dark, oak staircase as slowly and calmly as he could, feeling that he looked like someone from a Somerset Maugham novel, except for his hair. Little of the outside heat had penetrated the thick walls of the house and stepping outside was like being back in the tropics. Or he could have been entering the hothouse at Kew. It seemed a long time since he had gone there and had his vision of Melody's bottom. He went round to the terrace, keeping his hands in his pockets to stop himself wringing them. He paced up and down the rose garden, hungrily smoking one last cigarette. The roses were fading but there was a fine, dark bloom against the wall of the house and he tried to pick it for a buttonhole. When he touched it, the petals dropped to the ground. It did not matter. He searched and found a white one that was more resilient and smelt of honey which made him think of his favourite word, mellifluous. He stooped to read the label that Valentina had attached so thoughtfully. It was called Gabriel something or other and this pleased him.

There had been a shift in his heart. He felt lighter, as though he were breathing new air. For one whole night after Valentina had told him that Melody was coming to the party he had slept deeply and soundly. Since then he had tossed and turned as he mulled over every last detail. Valentina had told him that he should just let things happen, but only this afternoon the electrician had expressed grave doubts about the idea of fairy lights in the cypress trees. In less than an hour, he would see her. Valentina had said if it hadn't been for supporting Fitch, then the play would be best avoided. He only thought of Melody's face, smiling at him at last. But already, just from being outside for a few minutes, he felt the heat weighing him down. He had planned to walk but as he passed his parked car on the drive, he remembered its air-conditioning and got in.

He arrived in Illerwick with half an hour to spare. He didn't want to go to the school just yet, not wanting to be the first to arrive, so he parked the car higher up the main street and got out to stretch his legs. He thought he would sit outside The

Crown and have a pint. It would be a nice, summery thing to do and it would quell his nerves. He went in. It was empty, except for a dark-eyed man in the corner whose trousers were tied up with twine and who raised his glass to Leo sombrely. Leo couldn't place him. Ellie Swales was serving behind the bar. She said she was filling in for Jack and Mary who had already left for the play. She had got her invitation to the party, so being served took longer than he thought and no sooner had he sat down in the beer garden than he thought it was time to go. He had lost his appetite for the beer anyway. Now something strange was happening to the light. He looked behind him and a vast purple cloud was blocking the sky. Somewhere behind the cloud was a luminous, green tinge. The leaves had started to rustle.

When he went back through the pub, Ellie said, 'It's going to piss down, any minute.'

But when he got out onto the pavement, it still seemed curiously hot, as if the heat were coming up through the ground. The strong sun had gone but he thought he could just about get away with wearing his sunglasses. His jacket he carried carefully over one arm. He knew everyone would be looking at him because of the party. He decided to just beam and say 'See you there!' With his shades on, he could look around him more easily. He ran through several possible greetings in his head for when Melody materialised. He followed the groups of people towards the gates and showed his ticket. Children in costumes were running secretly through the crowd. The sensible people had brought umbrellas. He recognised Mr Boase up on a ladder in the middle of the trees with someone else who could have been the caretaker. They seemed to be tying plastic sheeting over the boughs of the trees like an awning. The stage itself was similarly cocooned, but in brightly coloured material with garlands of flowers on it. It looked like a beautiful cave. The first spots were falling as he reached the end of the play-ground, releasing the smell of the earth. As he found his seat, a band of minute children came on like a tribe of mice and started playing recorders. A rumble of thunder turned all eyes to heaven.

Settled in his seat, Leo looked around more. Reluctantly, he took off his sunglasses. The draped material from the trees formed a backstage area and he supposed she must be behind the curtain all the time. Perhaps she was watching him. He wondered if there was time to have a cigarette before the play started. It had become prematurely dark now because the rain was falling steadily. Most of the audience was covered by the plastic sheets but some people were standing on the edges with golfing umbrellas and cagoules. Everywhere people were saying what a pity it was about the weather. He thought, this must not happen at my party. Thank heavens for the orangery. Then he realised that there was no sign of Valentina. He scanned the audience quickly. Had they walked past each other? Was she waiting for him by the gate? But the recorders were stopping and Orsino was coming onto the stage.

If music be the food of love, play on,
Give me excess of it, that, surfeiting,
The appetite may sicken, and so die.

He knew the words off by heart. He felt them unravel in his memory. There was something in these young voices against the sound of the rain and just being here in Illerwick with all the people whom he had known since he was a child, that made tears come into his eyes. A flash of lightning was followed by a few little screams but bravely the children went on with their speeches and Orsino was led away to his sweet beds of flowers. The play delighted Leo. He thought about how he would find Melody at the end and congratulate her. Once, he thought about Valentina. Was she somewhere in the rain waiting for him? Had there somehow been crossed wires?

The rain fell steadily all through the first half. In the interval, people huddled together like sheltering birds or made mad dashes across the playground. Mr Boase appeared wearing a sou'wester and ferried pots of tea around. Leo stayed in his seat and chatted to people about the party. He saw Fitch's face peer out of the cave and they caught each other's eyes.

Leo said, 'Valentina?' Fitch shook his head.

He saw Fitch wave at the small, dark man he had seen in the pub who, he realised, must be his father. Melody did not appear. Only once did he see a figure in a too-large waterproof run past but it could have been anyone.

The show went on. Leo enjoyed waiting for the

lines that he remembered from when he was at school. He had laughed at Sir Andrew's '*I was adored once too*' in the first half. But during the last act the rain got even heavier. You could see it sweeping in darkly from the mountains. It was a serious storm and it was getting closer. The voices of the children grew thinner and reedier as the thunder and lightning increased, but no one for a moment lost concentration or seemed as though they would give up. The audience was swept up in the race to get the play finished before they were all struck by lightning. Even the tarpaulin collapsed but people just held it up around the edges for Fitch's last song:

> *When that I was and a little tiny boy*
> *With hey, ho, the wind and the rain . . .*

The audience was clapping and cheering and laughing and crying. As Fitch sang the very last words of the song, there was an enormous clap of thunder. Everyone ran for cover, screaming, grabbing their things and racing to their cars or running off down the streets with their coats over their heads. Leo thought he saw Melody in the rain, her face lit up by lightning. He called to her but she did not seem to hear. He ran after someone he thought was her but it turned out he was mistaken. He ran up the street to his own car. He had no choice. He sat inside the car with the rain beating on the roof and he rested his head on the steering wheel. There had been no proper ending. Halfway home, through tears and rain, he saw a sodden Valentina. He pulled up and she got in.

'I assumed it would be cancelled,' she said. They drove on.

'Did you know Patrick the gardener is still alive and coming to the party?'

'Blimey,' he said.

50
FITCH

It was the first day of the holidays and they were coming back from the sea on the bus. Yesterday they had all been talking about the play and whether it had been a success in spite of the storm or because of it, everyone saying remember when I . . . when you . . . when we . . . when the rain, when the lightning. Now, it was history. But being in the play had held them together. Fitch wondered what would happen now. Everyone was burnt and had wet, salty hair. They sat facing one another: Dave, Jimmy, Pete, Pauline, Lou and Suzy in a double seat each because the bus was empty. Through the bus windows the sea stretched out before them and so did the holiday.

But now, Fitch felt that he been cheated. People were saying that Pete and Suzy were 'an item'. It had all been because of the play. Now, he thought, I will have no one to talk to, but what was actually happening was that they were talking to him more, as though by talking to him they could talk to each other. They talked through him. When he saw either of them on their own, things were awkward.

Now that Fitch couldn't have Suzy, he wanted her. Suzy herself seemed perfectly aware of this. She looked at him triumphantly.

And then there was Miss Vye's note. Delivering the note had made him feel used but the worst thing was wanting to tell someone what he had found out. In the end, he did. They were back at the weir drinking cider and he just told them.

'So what you are saying,' said Pete, 'is that Vye is a dyke.'

'Looks like it.'

'So what?' Suzy said. 'It doesn't change anything.'

'Suppose not.'

'Surprising, really, though.' Fitch tried to sound casual.

Pete sighed. 'You see, Fitch, this is why you should never read other people's letters.'

And it was almost left at that, except that while they were on the subject of letters, quite out of the blue, Suzy said she had an idea of another little trick they could play on Boase, now that he had his invitation.

The next day, Fitch had to go to Beech House. He found Valentina in the kitchen garden. She had both hands on the barrow so she didn't wave and when he got close he saw that she was in a foul mood. He didn't blame her. He knew she hadn't been to the play.

'Best get things tidy,' she said, almost to herself, methodically clearing the storm damage.

He followed her around helplessly, waiting to be told what to do. She took him round the whole garden, showing him everything that was being done for the party: the lights, the special arrangements in pots, the area where the marquee was going to be. She told him they were going to rig up little ropes to stop people going into the parts of the garden that they didn't want them to see. She listed all the jobs that would have to be done during the week. She seemed to be telling him things he didn't need to know. He kept thinking, it's not as if I'm going to be in charge.

She sent him off on dead-heading duty but he didn't feel like doing any work. After an hour, he asked if they could have a break and to his surprise she immediately said, 'OK' and dropped her rake and gloves where she was standing on the path.

He followed her to the stable, waiting on the step until she had made the tea. There was no sign of Leo although his car was on the drive. She brought out the tea and saw him looking up at the house.

'His curtains are still drawn,' she said.

She looked pale and tired, but at least her hair was growing now.

'What's the matter?' he said.

'Nothing.'

She started picking the dried mud out of the bottom of her boot with a stick. A bit flew up and landed in his lap.

'I'm leaving,' she said.

He wasn't surprised. 'Have you told Leo?'

She shook her head.

'Don't you want to go?'

She went inside and got a cigarette. While she

was inside, the sun came out and made everything shine inappropriately.

'Wanting doesn't seem to have anything to do with it,' she said from inside a plume of smoke.

Then he remembered the party.

'You don't mean, you're going to leave him in the lurch right before the party?'

'I can do whatever I like,' she said.

She kept up this defiant talk for a while, then she just seemed to crumble against the wall. Fitch did not know what to do. He tried patting her as if she was one of the dogs. Then Valentina told him that she loved Leo and that she was a writer masquerading as a gardener. She said she came to Illerwick on impulse because her twin brother had gone to Sri Lanka and he had broken a promise. She said she hadn't told anyone else any of this, except Melody knew about the writing. Then she told him about Melody.

When she got to the part about the note she said, 'And she must have come here herself with that note. I thought she was supposed to be running a school, not haring about the countryside with love letters.'

Fitch shook his head, as though outraged.

'What a mess,' he said. 'You can't just leave, though. Think about it. What's he going to do without you?'

'I don't care any more.'

'Yes you do.'

'I just can't stand it. They're both as mad as each other.'

'I'll tell you what. Just stay for the party. It's only a party. She can't do anything. Have you tried actually telling Leo? About how you . . . um . . . feel about him?' Fitch couldn't believe that the adults were getting themselves into this mess.

'What's the point?'

'Just don't leave before the party.'

They went back to work and didn't mention it again. Fitch wondered what sort of state Miss Vye was in. Didn't mental illness run in families? Would she do something stupid? Leo came out in the afternoon, all bleary-eyed, and kept pestering Valentina about things he had been told a million times.

On the way home, Fitch went past Miss Vye's house and tried to look in at her windows to check if she was in there but there was no sign of her. Perhaps she had gone away after all. It would be a sensible thing to do. Then he thought, no, she will not have gone away.

51
JONATHAN

Jonathan is walking by the sea. It is all he can hear. The beach is empty, except for a few coconut husks. He watches the waves build up their massive explosions of water. The rain is pocking the sand and turning it drab. Behind him, the coconut trees are head-banging in the wind. He watches his feet corrupting the blank sand. It is hard to walk straight because of the wind and because of the slope of the sand into the water and because he was drinking arrack all last night. There are no fishing boats out today. There is no anything. Even the café on stilts higher up the beach is all shut up. He gets to the end of the beach and turns round. He plays a game of retracing his steps but his footmarks keep dissolving into the watery sand. He stumbles and falls down onto his knees just as quite a big wave is coming in. It washes him in. It feels strangely warm. He sits there laughing at himself and all the water seeps into his shorts and he thinks he might as well go for a little swim, ride the next wave. Hardly any way in at all, it's like stepping off a shelf. How deep it is under the water, he doesn't know.

It could be as deep as the Grand Canyon. He lets the waves push him around – to and fro, to and fro. He is suspended in their elastic motion and as they rise so does he and they carry him in and try to deposit him on the beach. Every few waves there is a surreally huge one. Some are like walls and they can pull you under and toss you round like you're in a washing machine. When your head comes up you are coughing and struggling for breath. The rain is getting harder and there is loud thunder booming above him.

52

MELODY

Melody remembered Valentina's words, '*I must down to the seas*'. She got in the car and drove to Breakers Point. She sat in the car park, surrounded by baking cars, and was afraid to get out. There was an ice-cream van and a man in a white coat in charge of the cars. Gabriel would have made a joke about this but she couldn't think of one. She was facing the cliff. It wasn't far really, across the field. She saw that a scroll of barbed wire had been put up, as if that would stop anyone. Nothing stops you if you really want to do it. Gabriel always said that. Every few minutes, with a roller-coaster lurch of her stomach, she was back on Bryn Mawr holding out her arms and saying those stupid words.

There were lots of people moving around with beach paraphernalia and ice-creams. At last, she did get out of the car and she walked about. She looked everywhere for her. She kept making a mistake and thinking that she had asked her to meet her by the sea, not after the play. She thought, why doesn't she come? She could not quite remember what she had said in the letter now. Everyone ignored her. She was no more important than a grain of sand. I shouldn't be here alone, she thought. She walked towards the cliff path. There were professional walkers coming along briskly.

One man said, 'Good afternoon!'

My brother killed himself here, she replied but he didn't hear her.

The heat was crushing her. All the thunderstorm had done was clear the air so it could get even hotter. There was no sea breeze. There had not ever been no sea breeze. She stood for a long time looking out at the waves coming in and in and hearing Valentina's voice caught up in them. It should have been Gabriel's voice. She thought: I wanted to kiss her.

She could not say why she felt the way she did about Valentina. She could not say why Gabriel had jumped off this cliff. She did not know the answers to anything. She did not know why she was always thinking of her and forgetting to think about him. She hated Leo. It was obvious that he had stolen Valentina's love.

Far away, she heard someone calling. She reached out instinctively for the barbed wire. How irritating that someone should be calling her now. Melody. Melody. Her name. She hated her name. It could be Valentina. Had she come? She turned back and saw a figure approaching. The figure was running. It wasn't her. It was a boy. She felt his arms around her waist. They pulled her clear and on to the ground. She was lying on the ground with her ear against the prickly grass. Someone was screaming.

The boy's arms were like steel around her. They did not move. She saw his face, his waxy skin, his carved mouth. She saw tears pulsing from the close eyes. She reached out a hand and caught one.

She stroked his face. 'It's OK,' she said.

'I thought you were going to die,' he said.

'No, Fitch, I wouldn't do that.'

She helped him up and they walked to the car with their arms around each other.

'Shhhh,' she said.

53

MR BOASE

Mr Boase was out in the sunshine. He was in the little park by the war memorial admiring the busy lizzies and the lobelia and the geraniums, letting his eye be drawn, insect-like, from colour to colour. The pollen scents from the flowerbeds flew up to his nostrils, or was it still her perfume he could smell? In his hand was a sheet of cream Basildon Bond. He took a long sniff. She had sprayed it with her perfume, only lightly, but it was definitely there. He did not know what it was called, only that it made him think of lilies of the valley and icing sugar. When she walked past him in the corridor at school or brushed near him in the staffroom it had always made him swoon. His eye roved from the ornamental beds to the flashing chrome of the parked cars on the road. For the first time in his life, he saw beauty everywhere. He was in a trance. He closed his eyes, just where he stood on the path. He relived the moment when he had opened the letter, as though he were watching himself on television. It had come that morning with the rest of the post. He had been stone cold sober. He had been standing in his pyjamas in the hall. This time there was no doubt about the writing on the envelope. He would recognise her italics anywhere. But the best moment was the moment when he had opened it and the smell had come flooding into his dark hallway like light. That was something he knew he would never forget as long as he lived.

When he left the house, he was a child again, running down the street. He did not know where he was going but he was filled with a surging energy that could have taken him anywhere. It could have taken him straight to her house, to her bedroom, to her bed. But, he said to himself, it is fools who rush in. I must bide my time. His celebratory drinks in the pub at lunchtime had left him humming the tunes from the jukebox and wanting to dance along the tarmac paths and all over the grass that said you should keep off it. Feeling his cheeks hurt with smiling, he hurried to a place in the shade by the box hedge and sat on a secluded bench. He unfolded the letter. Already the words were in his heart. His heart was a golden box and inside it he had stored these precious words like jewels. He thrust the letter into his innermost pocket. He did not need to read it again. When he closed his eyes, it was there, hovering beneath his lids, as clear as a photograph, down to the last exquisite stroke of her handwriting. He ran into a pool of sunshine. He threw down his blazer on the grass and lay in the sun like a mad dog with his newspaper over his face. He did not care who saw him. He let his fantasies run riot.

As soon as he got home, he started planning his

costume. It went without saying that there was nothing in his wardrobe that would do. He went and got the phone book and flicked through it with shaking hands. What he needed was a specialist shop. At last, he found one and explained his requirements. The people in the shop were very helpful. They said he could come in and try on as many costumes as he liked. He said he knew what he was looking for. He made an appointment for the next day. He had calculated that it would be an hour's drive each way and he would need an early lunch and no beer if he were to survive the ordeal. This was the least sacrifice he could make. He liked the idea of making a sacrifice for her.

That night he could not sleep for thinking about her, for thinking about the moment they would meet in the magical garden at Beech House that he had never seen. He saw himself saying, 'I always knew', her eyes shining and looking into his, both of them disguised but truly themselves at last.

54
JONATHAN

The sun on Jonathan's face woke him. He didn't open his eyes. He could feel himself rocking from side to side. He was in a boat but the sea seemed far distant. He let his hand fall over the side of the boat but it fell into air. There was the smell of pineapple juice, cigarette smoke and frying onions. Somewhere people were arguing loudly in Sinhala. As far as he could tell, the subject of their argument was a broken plate. He opened his eyes and they focused painfully on a mesh of leaves high above. Behind them was a hot sky. He breathed in but it was like a gulp of water going down the wrong way and he started coughing. He couldn't stop the coughing. He could hardly breathe at all. A man was standing beside him, silhouetted. He recognised him but could not remember his name. The man hit him on his back. It seemed to work. Something came into his mouth, like watery vomit. He spat it out and lay back down.

'That's probably the last of it,' someone said.

The man swung the hammock gently as if it were a cradle. Jonathan's throat was raw.

'Do you remember anything?'

He thought, yes, I remember the two of us, running along the sand. Running from end to end of the beach through the edge of the sea and the way the water slapped and whipped at our legs. Dad told us we were too young to swim and we mustn't go in the water or we might drown. He shook his head. He tried to ask the man his name but no sound came out.

The man brought a coconut. He remembered these. *Thambili*. His head was pounding and he drank the coconut water sideways through the straw.

'You nearly drowned, mate. Had to jump in and pull you out myself. You were drunk as a skunk.'

There was anger in his voice. Jonathan wanted to hide from this anger bearing down on him like the tall shadow of a man he didn't know.

'You've been out for the count for three hours.'

Jonathan saw himself as if from heaven walking along the sand. He saw his footprints. He saw two sets of footprints merging and then wending apart. He remembered the taste of the arrack and coke and wanted to throw up.

'I'm sorry,' he said. The man squeezed his hand. Jonathan remembered his name was Phil. Phil was angry because he cared about him.

He said, 'You saved my life.' But it sounded like a corny line from a film and they sniggered. 'Did you give me the kiss of life?'

'I can't believe you've blanked it out.'

He felt too hot, now. The sun lay across his chest in white bars. He didn't want to be a liability to this man, Phil, any more.

He sat up a bit. There were other people watching: some surfers leaning over a balcony. The guesthouse owner. All their faces were serious. In the shadows of the garden two Tamil maids were chatting about him in unsentimental voices as though he were dead.

Phil helped him out of the hammock. The sea was different now, as if the sea before had been another sea in another time and place. He tottered on the sand. Phil led him to the sea, rushing in small waves towards them. Was this something like being made to get straight on your bicycle when you fell off as a kid? Part of him wanted to shake off this man who had saved his life and who was angry because he cared about him. Part of him didn't want anyone to care about him any more. But he couldn't shake him off. He needed to hold on to someone. Phil led him into the water. They found a quiet channel. The waves soothed him. He floated. He leaned back gently and felt the water support the whole weight of his heavy head. All the time, Phil didn't let go. He held him in the water even though water is somewhere you cannot fall. Jonathan allowed his body to relax against him. He didn't care that he had nearly drowned or that he had forgotten that he had nearly drowned.

He went to his room while he was still wet, closed the shutters and lay in a green darkness, whipped cool by the fan. He slept and dreamed of being a child and when he woke up he was hungry. He could hear voices outside. People were playing a card game that he didn't understand. There were some girls there. He recognised the voice of a pretty Irish girl with dark brown hair that they had met one day by the *kadé*. Suddenly, he wanted to be near her, to listen to her talking and for her to smile at him and maybe even kiss her. Because he was alive! He had nearly died but Phil had saved him and he was alive! He tried to dress hurriedly, blundering around in the room, looking for long trousers and a shirt, but halfway into his clothes, he abruptly sat on the bed. He was starting to remember. A tall wave. Dark struggling. He slowed back down. He smoked a cigarette. He lit a mosquito coil. By the time he got outside, they weren't even playing the game any more, they were just talking. The sky was blue-black and full of stars. The lights on the balcony lit up the leaves. He realised that it must have rained heavily again earlier because the ground was damp, but he hadn't even heard it. He had been asleep for hours. The girl smiled at him and he sat down beside her.

She turned to him. 'We've all been talking about why we're here?' She was slightly drunk or stoned. They all were, he could see that now.

He ate some bread that had been left on the table. It was too late to order any food. No one else seemed to be listening. Phil was stroking the hair of another girl that Jonathan had never seen. She was sitting on his lap.

'I, for example, split up with my boyfriend,' she was saying.

Phil interrupted her. He said, 'Jonathan used to live here when he was a kid.'

Everyone turned and looked at him and made little murmuring noises. Then the sea hushed them.

He looked at them all in the chiaroscuro light.
His throat felt bruised.

He said, 'I broke a promise.'

When he went back to his room, everything felt
very clear in his mind.

He moved in there all in the ghost-story light.
The almost-dark moved.
He said, 'I wrote a tribute.'
[illegible] Davis went back to his room. Something [illegible]
was close to his head.

55

MR BOASE

They had packed the costume in a flat cardboard box. He carried it in from the car and laid it carefully on his bed. The suit part was wrapped in plastic and then there was a little bag with the wig and the make-up which he had had to buy, not hire. The long shoes were wedged at the bottom of the box and stuffed with newspaper. He drew the curtains and switched on the light. He wondered what he should wear underneath. Perhaps nothing. He had only black socks and he felt these were not quite right. Perhaps he should purchase some brighter ones. He took off his vest and underpants and pulled on the stretchy outfit. Built into its lining was a padded stomach. It was all very simple. He practised moving around in it. He had to be careful when he sat down that the stomach didn't get pushed up under his chin. The colours shocked him. He had never worn anything that was not an ordinary colour like beige or grey or navy. In his whole life, he had stuck to ordinariness. He opened the wardrobe door and appraised the effect. It was a surprisingly good fit. Next, he put the shoes on.

These were the things that really needed practice. At first it was impossible but after a while he managed a sort of lolloping stride that took him from one side of the bedroom to the other. The wig was orange. He put it half on as though it were a hat to get an impression of how he would look and laid out the greasepaints on his chest of drawers. Then he put everything back in the box.

That night, he fell asleep on the sofa. Shuffling to his bed in the early hours he knew that he should stop drinking. He thought of her, only a stone's throw away. He wondered if she was asleep. Was she thinking of him as he was thinking of her? He imagined her lying beside him in the bed where no one had ever lain. He got up and took a peek at the costume lying in the bottom of the wardrobe. It symbolised a new Boase. He would be a success at the party. He would be a success at his job. For once in his life, he would be a success. I can't stop smiling, he thought as he felt himself slipping into sleep.

In the morning he phoned up the local florist and asked them to send her a single red rose. A rose from Boase.

56
LEO

It was two evenings before the party. Leo was inspecting the garden. Everything that could be ready now, was ready now. He wanted to trace Melody's footsteps on the night of the party. He imagined she would be arriving through the beech woods and he walked towards them. The height of summer had passed. He could detect the faintest hint of a chill in the air, which made him think of September and then autumn. He knew that autumn was an important time for the garden and that many new things could be planted. With the heat gone, he felt that more could be achieved. He tried to imagine that something would have changed by then. It would not be the same as now. He knew that at least. He walked across the lawn and then turned and began walking back the way he had come, this time with the house before him and everything that she would see.

The barometer in the hall had said changeable. He thought, it will be an evening like this. As he walked past the big beech tree that they used to sit under, he saw an owl on its lower branches, its feathers ruffling delicately, and he wondered how long owls lived. It hooted and sailed diagonally towards the woods. As he looked across at the terrace, he tried to see with her eyes. He tried to envisage the terrace alive with people. He imagined the flash of the silver trays of the hired waiters in the low sunlight, the steady rise of voices as she got nearer. Would she remember? Should he stand where he had stood once before? People would be walking in ones and twos into the rose garden. Still now, there were some surviving blooms. He turned to walk along the highest of the terraced walks, deliberately brushing past the box hedge with his legs, so it would release its pungency. The Japanese anemones were out. A blue clematis. Some purple geraniums. Their petals were luminous as if there were candles behind them.

On the level below, the orangery was ready. He could smell the orange trees. He crushed a leaf between his fingers. There were two long tables already laid with green cloths for the drinks, a few chairs from the house. There was a space where a violin quartet would be playing, four old friends from music college who had been lured by the idea of a party. They would be arriving tomorrow; he slightly feared them. He closed the door and stood for a moment looking down at the lower lawns and the lily pond. The marquee men would be coming tomorrow too. That was where the hub of the party would be and where all the dancing would go on. Jack Flagg had got someone to DJ. He had hauled down all the old boxes of his parents' records for him to look at. He wondered if it would help. He wondered if Melody might remember some of the old songs. He tried to imagine himself holding her in his arms.

In the kitchen garden, he caught sight of Valentina sitting on a low brick wall.

'All this should be dug over,' she said matter-of-factly.

She seemed in a rather odd mood.

'What are you doing?' he said.

'Nothing much.'

He sat down next to her and offered her his ciga-rette case. When he lit her cigarette, the flame lit up the sadness in her face.

'I want you to enjoy yourself at this party,' he said. 'No work.'

They went for a stroll. Valentina tested him on his plant knowledge, which was improving. His new terminology consisted of crocosmia, potentilla and datura. She always laughed at the way he pronounced the names of flowers and she laughed now. He liked this feeling.

She said, 'Leo?'

He stopped and looked at her across the sundial. Her eyes looked strange. He thought of lapis lazuli. Her hair was like a bird's crest. She was like some strange, inquisitive bird of paradise in his garden. Suddenly, he felt that he had not cherished her. She seemed so fragile and she had done all this hard work while all he had done was mope around. He walked round the side of the sundial and put his arms around her very tightly. She felt warm and fluttery against his chest. He heard himself make a little noise, like a sigh. Or perhaps it was Valentina who made the noise. He kissed the top of her crest. She smelt of mown grass.

'Thank you for everything,' he said.

He pushed away her shaking body and held her at arm's length.

'I should be throwing this party just for you and all your hard work!' He laughed madly. They stood awkwardly on the path. He looked away when she started wiping her nose on the sleeve of her overall. She went to gather her tools and he stood waiting for her near the apple trees. It was dusk and the sky was full of bats. He loved bats.

'Valentina?' he called but she had gone.

57

VALENTINA

Before she got dressed, Valentina propped up a spotted mirror she had found and studied herself. She had lost weight and her body had a carved look. She put her arms around her own body. She thought of Leo. She touched her hair where he had kissed her. It had been then that she had decided, with her head against his shirt, feeling the pressure of his mouth on her hair. She would stay for the party and then go. She would leave him a letter to explain. Or she would go to where he would be playing the piano and tell him, the taxi waiting, so he could do nothing about it. Or she would tell him at the party, at the end of the party in a quiet moment, looking at the stars from the terrace. She did not know what she would do, she only knew that the night of the party would be her last at Beech House and it was unbearable. But then a wave of panic rushed through her. Wildly, she tipped out the contents of her suitcase that she had packed and repacked so many times in the last few days and looked at the dull heap that resulted. She put on some jeans and a T-shirt. She went to the window and sat for a long time staring at the sheep. Then she walked across the yard to the house.

The front door was wide open. Leo was playing the blues in the drawing room in a great beam of sunlight, his cigarette balanced on the treble keys. She stood watching him, trying to think of what to say, trying not to think that soon he would no longer be part of her life. She knocked.

'Yeah?' he said, without looking, in a blues kind of voice.

'It's me.'

'Who?' Still he kept on playing and not looking. He took a quick drag.

She went and stood by his shoulder. He stopped.

'Valentina.' He seemed discomfited but then he smiled and got up and started to move towards the hall and the front door, which was still open, assuming it was garden or party business. She thought, I just have to say this. There are other avenues to try if it doesn't work.

She touched his arm to bar him from going through the door.

'Leo?'

'Yes?'

'Um. I haven't a thing to wear for the party.'

He was dumbstruck. Then flustered. 'Oh. I see. Umm.'

'I should have bought something. It's too late. I didn't think. I don't really know why I'm asking you.'

He smiled kindly. 'Don't worry. Let me think. Of course, you should have something special. Tell you what, there's a great big wardrobe full of clothes in the blue room. My mother kept all her dresses in it. Didn't know what to do with them.' He looked at her doubtfully. 'She was a bit taller than you.'

He led the way and she followed him up the musty stairs. He opened the door and she went in first. She looked at the hand-painted wallpaper, the blue coverlet, the view of the rose garden.

'What a beautiful room!' she said.

He looked away and coughed strangely. He opened a gigantic mahogany wardrobe. A moth flew out.

'You might find something,' he said, stepping back and flicking his ash unceremoniously into the fireplace. 'They sort of go down the ages.'

They both stood before the open door of the wardrobe, which was bulging with coloured swathes of material. He stepped forward and touched something which changed colour as he moved it back and forth in the light. Taffeta. They smiled. She slipped her hand inside the cool gills of the side-by-side dresses. They smelt of old parties and stale perfume. She heard his footsteps creaking away down the landing and then the piano starting again downstairs.

She started to get the dresses out, to lay them carefully on the bed with the blue coverlet. Some full-skirted ones were obviously fifties dresses. Others were kaftans, slippery silk strapless gowns, even mini-dresses with plastic hoops around the midriff and in the bottom of the wardrobe were white boots and pointed stilettos and gold sandals with flowers on the side. They could have gone in a museum as classic examples of dresses from the last five decades. She picked them out one by one and held them against her. She must have had a lot of panache to wear these, she thought. But I should just pick anything. It doesn't matter what I look like. Any dress will do. She started trying them on. The fabrics were irresistibly expensive: satin, velvet, crêpe de Chine, silk, taffeta. Many of them were white or cream like forlorn wedding dresses. She tried on a long gown encrusted with glass beads and gasped at herself. She walked up and down. She took it off. She buried her head in the wardrobe and saw a bluey-green colour like a tropical sea. She pulled it out gently and held it against her. It looked a strange shape on the hanger; it seemed to have a sort of bustle and a little train like a mermaid's tale. It was made of taffeta and the darknesses in it were like the shadows of waves in the sea. The bodice was hard and shaped like a heart and seemed to be made out of a shell that had been broken in half. It almost fitted. She would have to take a tuck here and there. She found some silver shoes, which were too big, but she could stuff them with tissue paper. There were some mother of pearl hair combs which might stick in her hair if she was lucky. She got changed and stuffed everything into a Biba carrier bag she found in the bottom of the wardrobe. She tiptoed through the hall, past Leo's piano playing. She didn't want him to see her. Not yet. She wanted him to see her transformed. There was only one more thing to do before the party, and that was to visit Patrick.

Patrick was sitting with the others listening to the news at maximum volume but when he saw her standing by the window, he came over to her in a strange little running movement. Then he sat down for a while and caught his breath. His cardigan was buttoned up wrong, but apart from that, he seemed chirpy.

'All ready for tomorrow?' she said.

'Gat me tayuls. Glyn. He gat um for me in Porth Gwyn. Only second 'and they are, see. Never 'ad tayuls before.'

'Brilliant! There's a taxi coming for you at six forty-five tomorrow.' She gave him a piece of paper with 6.45 p.m. written on it in black marker and he put it shyly in his pocket.

'There's a sort of wheelchair at the house. I'm going to push you round in that.'

'At th'owze? That old thing? That's a bath chair, that is.'

'Don't worry. You won't fall out.'

He looked doubtful. She touched his arm and he patted her hand with his gnarled one. When she looked back at the window he was standing up, holding his arm high as if she were going on some great voyage instead of a few miles down the road. All the time Beech House was minutes away, but he had not seen it for years.

She took a route through Illerwick which avoided Melody's house. Fitch was cycling round in circles near The Crown.

'Still here, then?' he said.

'Until Sunday.'

'Cool. See you at the party,' he said and cycled off.

When she got back, Leo was standing in the courtyard looking up at the sky. He looked back down and their eyes met.

'Find anything?' he said.

'Yes,' she said. 'Thanks.'

'Good. Marquee's up.'

'Patrick's all set.'

'Chin up,' he said, in a weird voice, almost as if to himself, and went inside.

She went and had a look at the marquee and stood in the middle of it and heard the wind drumming on the outside like the overture to some strange opera. She would be going in less than two days' time, back to the empty flat in Finsbury Park and to yet another job in yet another bookshop. Then she would think of this as a dream.

When she went past Leo's study, it was empty. She looked up at the room where she knew he slept. The curtains were drawn but there were chinks of light.

Probably trying on his outfit, she thought.

Oh, Leo.

It was his birthday tomorrow. She went and got the card she had bought from Betty's shop and slipped it through the letterbox. Then she went back to the stable and prayed that Melody would keep her promise and talk to him. She prayed that Leo would be all right. She tried to blank out all thoughts of loving him.

58

FITCH

When Fitch had left Valentina, he had cycled off in the direction of his cottage but that was all. Then he had climbed onto the roof of the telephone box and looked over Melody's wall to see if she was all right. He had been doing this for several days. So far, so good. She was sitting in her garden on a blue blanket reading a book and drinking wine. She had been doing this for several days. He watched her for a few minutes, then he rode back into town. He cycled round The Crown car park twice. He didn't really know what he was doing. He went to the end of Suzy's road. After a while she came out of her house.

'Hi,' she said.

'Hi.' Fitch leaned his bike against someone's garage wall. 'Fancy a walk?' he said.

'OK.' Neither of them asked the other where they were going. They just walked behind the houses where Suzy lived, over a stile and into a field full of thistles and cowpats which led to the sewage works. The cows were huddled in a corner. Fitch wanted to ask her what was going on with Pete.

He said, 'What've you been up to lately?'

'Nothing much. Hanging around with Pete. My mum's gone to Spain.'

'Cool.' What did she mean, hanging around? What was that supposed to mean?

They were walking about a metre apart, which was how it had come to be between them, now. She looked pretty, as usual. Her hair was let down from its ponytail, as shiny as glass. He ran his fingers through it in his mind. She told him that they had seen Boase going mad over the letter in the park.

Fitch said, 'That'll teach him.'

She said, 'Don't seem to have seen much of you lately.' She dodged a horsefly.

'I'm sorry. I've been busy.'

They walked with their heads down through a cloud of gnats. One of the cows bellowed.

'They're not bulls, are they?' he said.

'I don't think so. Um. I'd better go back now.'

'Oh, OK.' It was too soon.

They walked in silence, back through the maze of thistles and cowpats. At the stile, she lost her balance slightly and touched his hand. It felt like an electric shock. He thought, I have to ask her now. It is my last chance. He looked at her face with the sunset shining directly into it. She was screwing up her eyes, which gave the illusion that she was smiling but he knew she was not.

Suddenly, he couldn't stand it any more.

He said, 'Bye then!' and ran to get his bike. As he ran towards it he saw that a dog was weeing on it.

'Fitch!'

He turned to see her standing at the edge of her

crazy paving with her hand up as though she was trying to lasso him.

'Come here, a minute.'

He ran back and she pulled him towards her and bumped her lips clumsily against his. A mighty cheer went up in all the neighbouring streets and gardens, but only Fitch heard it.

'See you at the party!' she said.

'Definitely,' he said.

Now he was too happy to go home. He kept on and on cycling even though it was nearly dusk. He thought, it is such a lovely evening. It is still warm. It is a balmy evening. Barmy. People should be out and about enjoying themselves, but there was no one. They were probably all watching *EastEnders*. Then he saw, in the distance, Valentina again. She seemed to be getting out of a taxi, which was odd. He rode towards her, but it was not her. It was a man. He was standing near the bus shelter with a scrap of paper in his hand, which he was turning round and round and then turning and experimentally facing in different directions. He looked dizzy. Fitch stopped near him and pretended to be fixing something on his bike.

'Excuse me,' came an almost familiar voice. Fitch looked at the man's blond hair and his sharp, blue eyes. He knew immediately who he was. He went over.

'I'm looking for Beech House?' he said, Aussie-style.

Never, for the rest of Fitch's life, did he know why he did what he did next.

'Go to the bridge down there. Then you have to go up the riverbank. It's sort of along the ends of people's gardens, but it doesn't matter. No one minds. When you come to a willow tree, you will know you're at the right place. I think the person you're looking for is in the garden.'

He hoped she still was.

'Oh, right, thanks?' The man looked nervous.

Fitch watched him go. He felt exhilarated. He cycled home incredibly fast and burst into the kitchen where his father was calmly frying potatoes. He gave him a spontaneous hug.

'What was that for, my boy?'

'Everything and nothing,' he said.

After supper, he went up to his cabin-room without turning on the light so he could see the stars and the lights outside. He thought, Illerwick is unlike anywhere else in the world. He thought, Suzy has never liked Pete. I know she has always wanted me.

59

MELODY

Each evening, she had been drawn outside into the soupy, insect-laden air, to the sounds of other people and traffic and to life going on beyond the cold, stone walls of the vicarage. Hidden in the garden, she could hear the river, and children arguing on the bridge, the splash of a stone. She tried to read. She tried to stop her mind playing a continuous spool of everything that had happened and had not happened. It was like a cine film that had been taken of them on the beach once by her father's curate, Mr Petrie. Gabriel always wanted to play it again and again because everything always seemed too fast. Because there were no sounds or words and you had to read the faces. It was precious time. Time caught, captured like a fish. It showed you things you hadn't seen the first time round.

It had all started when he came home from London. His face looked ill. He frightened her. She saw gestures she had never seen him make before – a hand scraped through his hair, a cracking of his knuckles. Or he lay like a shell on his bed in his high room at the top of the house and let the world wash over him. He kept wittering on about Leo but he never went to Beech House. She saw his mouth making the shape of Leo's name. He said he thought she secretly loved Leo. She said it wasn't true, but even if it were true, why should it matter? Why was he interfering with her life? He said, subconsciously, I said subconsciously, banging his fist down hard on the arm of the chair. She saw their arguments going round and round the house in different rooms, in mime, a mime of possession and madness and lost things. He went to the doctor. He laid out his pills on the arm of the chair like beads. He sat by the fire, drinking extravagantly. She told him what had happened on New Year's Eve. He trembled. He smiled. He didn't believe her. He hurled himself off a cliff.

In his place came a strange girl. She watched the girl's face, a heart. She said her name. She saw how she would be at the party. Her face that she had imagined a particular way under a certain kind of moonlight and the twist of their hands together as she led her through a sea of faces. These moments that would never actually occur. This is what she was watching in her mind. Leo was there, a stone statue on the edge of the terrace. He never moved from his position. She thought of that final party, all those summers ago. How he had been standing there waiting. She thought of Gabriel and Leo. Thick as thieves. She remembered Gabriel's excitement as they had walked through the wood, the way he always gabbled and jabbered when he was excited. Had the madness started then? Had no one noticed? That party was the last time they were ever close. Any of them. And yet it was a blur. A picture of some people dancing and then nothing. Then it was gone. Abrupt, like the end of the cine film.

The sun had gone from the garden now. The wine made her body sing and she wanted to stay there, not moving, just lying on her side on the cool earth, watching ants tumbling through the grass, or on her back, seeing the sky moving and cross-hatched with the flights of birds. The garden seemed to hold her safe, invisible, inside its shadows, screened by the willows and tall weeds. She took off all her clothes. She stretched her long body out and lay still on the rug as though she were asleep. All around her, she imagined the garden like a Rousseau painting.

There was a noise. It sounded like the splash of oars, steady and strong in the water. But it is not oars, she thought, it is the sound of wading. Someone is wading towards me. She could not move. She was a woman painted into a garden. Her eyes were shut. She held her breath, heard sounds that were not normally heard: willow leaves being parted, tiny scrapings of the edges of leaves and the catch of long thin boughs. Blades of grass being crushed by bare feet. Knees falling down before her. A hand that flew through the thick, scented air and landed on the bone of her hip. A face that came near hers. She felt its breathing, a panicky breath, then the hand on her head, like her father's giving blessing. She opened her eyes.

'You!' she said, then, 'No.'

He didn't say anything. He only looked. She drew the blanket round her.

'I thought you were dead,' he murmured. 'You looked as though you were dead.'

Her hands gripped the woollen folds of the blanket.

'Is Valentina here?'

No words came. She shook her head. He started to back away, towards the screen of willows, saying there had been a mistake, that someone had told him to come there. That he was sorry. He was tripping over the wet ends of his jeans, dropping a shoe and picking it up and then dropping it again and stooping down, his hair falling into his eyes.

'Wait,' she said.

He stood swaying. He came back. She told him the way to Beech House, the way through the woods. He watched her face as she told him and he nodded and said, 'I should go.' But he didn't go. He lay down on the grass and closed his eyes. Then he opened them and looked at her again. And when he did this she felt as if she were falling very fast through the air. He began to tell her a story. And even though all the time there was the feeling that he was just about to leave, he stayed there until it was night. He said that once upon a time, Sri Lanka was called Serendip and that's where the word serendipity comes from. He told her that there were once Three Princes of Serendip, who were always making happy discoveries by chance on their voyages in search of other things. All the time the feeling that he might leave was there, but he did not leave. The passion flowers clustered round him like stars. She moved closer to him, closer to the ebb and flow of his breathing.

She said, 'It's very dark, now, to go through the wood.'

He looked up at the vast velvety dome of the sky. 'Yes,' he said.

The river licked its reeds on the bank. She reached out her hand towards him and he folded it up inside his own, as though she were a happy discovery he did not want to leave. And she held his heart-shaped face between her palms, and she traced the familiar curve of his mouth with her finger.

60
JONATHAN

She showed him the way to Beech House the next day. He held her cool, white hand in his. She led him through the wood: dark, light, dark, light, the roar of the leaves like tides. They did not speak in words. They spoke through little movements and signs – the press of a thumb, the brush of their hips, the distance between them – the way it opened and closed. She took him to where the woods ended and the grounds of the house began. She held up their joint hands like one fist.

'I will leave you here,' she said and let him undo the knot of their fingers. He peeled them away, one by one. He held her face in his hands. He kissed the downy skin on the side of her arched neck, closing his eyes to the sound of the sea above him. He turned away. He stood still and heard behind him the crackling of her quick footsteps like fire as she ran back down the path. He imagined her red hair streaming behind her in the wind.

He crossed the wide, green space. He looked at the house, the windows seeming to him an expression of a face that disapproved of him. He saw a wedding marquee that was not. He saw people moving to and fro like beetles. He heard the sound of hammering, shouts in the air, the rev of an engine. He edged round the house. The gravel announced his presence. He saw a terraced garden. On a path, a knot of people, men with loud voices holding violins, a quiet man with his arms folded across his chest, stepping away from the group, smoothing his hair ineffectually. There was a building like a glass palace. The door opened. Valentina. He stopped because he saw that her hair had gone. He laughed at the sight of her. He called her name, 'Valentina!' It reverberated in the garden, against the glass, against the pots and the stone steps and further and further out into the hills. She turned. She ran shouting into his arms and he threw her up in the air and caught her again, an echo of himself.

They did not speak of what had happened. It was only the present that mattered now.

She said, 'You're alive.' Then she presented him to the assembled company. She stood to attention by his side in her proud way. The man with the curly hair came forward. The others stood with their violins hanging by their sides, their mouths open.

'Leo, this is my brother, Jonathan.'

'Twins!' said someone.

'Peas in a pod!'

Jonathan looked hard into her face. Beneath its surface, a terrible pain was lurking. He felt a twinge of pain in his own heart in response. This is what happens sometimes when you are a twin.

61
VALENTINA

Valentina had been in the orangery. Mary Jones from The Crown had been there, helping to set out glasses.

'I'm getting married,' she had said.

Valentina had congratulated her.

'It's because of the baby, really. I love him, though, my Jack.'

Valentina had thought, they think I am going to be here for ever. They do not think that there is a world outside. It is the last thing on anyone's mind that I should leave. She had looked at Leo through the glass and seen the familiar way his jacket strained across his back when he folded his arms. It was a matter of hours now. She wanted the other people to go away. She knew that they would not. She would never again be alone with him. It would just be this. Not being able to talk to each other. The necessity of being polite. She thought of smashing her fists through the glass. Now they would be coming in for their rehearsal. She would be expected to go away, to busy herself with other things. She was only the gardener.

Mary Jones had been saying something about the baby. Valentina had nodded and laughed. She had clenched her fists. She had to get outside. They had formed a little ring, shutting her out, shutting her out, shutting her out. She opened the door. She heard her name echo. Jonathan. She jumped up into his arms. He was alive. He was alive. She took him to show Leo. The violins drooped down.

'Twins!'

'Peas in a pod!' said the musician with the thick moustache.

She looked hard into Jonathan's face. Something momentous had happened to him. It was there in his eyes.

'Are you all right?' she said.

'Are you?'

62

JONATHAN

When they were alone in the stable, he told her. Valentina put her hands over her mouth. Underneath her hands she could have been smiling or her mouth could have been an open door of shock. Then she looked fierce. She gripped him by the hand, not caring that her nails were making sharp indentations in his palm.

'Leo must not find out.'

She did not say that she loved Leo. She chose to keep this in her heart. Something that could not be said. Jonathan understood this. He promised that Leo would not find out.

'Stay close to me,' she said. 'Make Melody be nice to Leo for your sake, if no one else's. If he finds out suddenly, there is no knowing what might happen.'

'Melody will be wondering where I am.' He stood at the stable door. He wanted to get back to her, to where she was waiting for him in her empty house. He thought of how the two of them together would fill the empty spaces with their voices. He wanted to hear the story of her life so he could take it up and stitch it to his own.

Valentina said, 'I'll see you later. You must be here early, say six-thirty. Let her come later.'

She hugged him. Then she said, 'Jonathan, how did you find me?'

He said, 'Miss Bratby.' Then he left.

240

63

VALENTINA

The afternoon sun had warmed the roof above her bed. She was sewing tucks in the dress. She thought: I will sew myself into it. She slipped on the silver shoes stuffed with tissue paper and held out her thin legs. She pulled some strands of hair away from her forehead. She took out her make-up bag and examined its contents.

64
LEO

The time had come. His thirtieth birthday. He stood before his oval looking-glass and tried to see something good in himself. He looked ugly but elegant. He could not contain all the things that he was feeling. He knew something had changed since the beginning but he could not quite put his finger on it. He did not know what he meant by the beginning. He felt too starched and smart. He jogged up and down the corridor, slipping and sliding in his polished shoes. He was glad there was no one there to see him. He went back and looked at his reflection. Now he was his more dishevelled self. He felt no better. He sighed, resigned himself to whatever might happen, and shut the bedroom door. As he came down the staircase, he became aware of the flurry of activity in the hall. The hired staff crisscrossed the tiles busily, as though they were used to these affairs. They had said they did weddings, mainly.

It was still really only late afternoon. Not much beyond teatime. But he had to be ready. Soon they would come. He stood on the upper level of the garden and thought of everyone else getting ready in Illerwick, in each mind the anticipation of the party. He almost wished that reality would never come. He thought of Melody, alone in her house, finally allowing herself to take pleasure in something. He held his face up to the sun, basking in its healing powers. That was what he wanted for Melody, he realised. For her to be healed. He saw a little grey cloud hovering above the distant mountains and prayed it would not rain. Everything was ready. He saw his friends, the musicians, coming towards him on the gravel path, full of bonhomie. He raised a jovial hand. They were talking amongst themselves, laughing heartily, going into the orangery to start tuning up. He heard the timbre of their voices changing, strange notes emerging from their instruments. He moved away through the sunlight and shade. He sat on the edge of the fountain and dabbled the water. All was quiet and waiting. He thought of some things, of being young here, then, with Melody in his arms so delicate and perfect. He walked around the tennis courts to the old summerhouse and sat inside its musty shell for longer than he should have done. Everything had changed; there was no going back to the old garden. He knew he was staying away from the terrace for too long. He wore no watch. He picked some cobwebs off his suit. Above him, far away on the highest level, he saw the white shapes of his first guests. As he moved closer, he heard the violin quartet playing in the orangery.

He took a glass of champagne from a passing tray

and sipped it, moving among people he knew and some he had never seen before in his life. He talked to Jack Flagg and congratulated him on his forthcoming marriage. He saw Fitch talking to Pete and the others who had been in the play. He heard her voice behind him.

'Happy Birthday, Leo.' She held out both her white-gloved hands. He moved towards them. She was smiling. She was wearing a black dress like a river of ink, her hair drawn back, her eyes shining. She was alone on the path. He put his free hand in hers and felt the white satin gloves close over his fingers. She was brimming with happiness.

'Melody!'

That she could be so happy, here and now! But something had changed. Something had changed but he did not like to think what it was because the consequences were too far-reaching.

She said, 'The garden looks wonderful, Leo.'

He noticed how easily she spoke his name. He took her arm and led her carefully along the paths as if he were afraid she would shatter into a million pieces. He showed her every plant that had been planted, every change that had been made.

Once, he saw her eyes fill with tears.

'That you should have done all this,' she said, gently.

He smiled. 'It is Valentina. It is all Valentina.'

'Where is she?' Leo cast about looking for her. Patrick! He remembered he had to be at the front entrance for seven to meet Patrick. Valentina would be there waiting for him. He glanced at Melody's watch and politely excused himself. He raced round the side of the house and crashed into something shimmering. It fell into his arms. He stepped back.

Valentina stood before him. He thought: she is an apparition. She smiled. She slowly made a revolution on the path so that her dress changed and changed in the light. The lights in it were like slippery scales. Her face. It was soft and blushing. She smiled. He stood and stared and in his hand her hand was still because he had forgotten to let go when they collided.

He dropped her fingers as though he had been burned. He could not speak of how she looked to him. He steadied himself on the wall.

He said, 'Is he here?'

'Yes! I was just coming to look for you.'

He thought he should take her hand. He thought of Melody. He did not take her hand. They walked in silence to the porch.

65

MR BOASE

The house was farther along the lane than he thought. There weren't any other cars about, which was surprising; he knew now that there were others in the town who had been invited but this was only to be expected for a man of Leo Spring's standing. He hoped he was not late. He checked the invitation. Eight o'clock. The others must be walking through the wood, but you couldn't see the wood from here. He imagined a procession of costumed figures among the trees, like people from a play. He was glad he had decided to make his entrance in style. He imagined Leo Spring greeting him on the house steps, whiskered and maned like a lion. Leo the lion. He chuckled to himself. The taxi driver was a man of few words but he had come punctually and everything was going to plan. Boase leaned back. He felt calm. Not drunk. Only a little Dutch courage inside him. Every now and then, as the car bumped along and his weight shifted, he caught a glimpse of his orange hair in the mirror or a flash of his white made-up face. The make-up felt sticky and heavy. Perhaps he had applied it too thickly? It had been a tricky business following the illustration on the back of the box.

The house came fully into view. He felt privileged to be entering its hallowed grounds. He took off his glasses and slipped them into a handy little pocket he had found in the bottom half of the nylon suit. The taxi stopped. He counted out the change carefully, passed it to the driver and gave him a little clown wave. But only when the car had reversed and had turned tail, did he snap on the elasticated red nose.

Everything was oddly deserted but he could hear the soft rise and fall of voices and music nearby. There was a white oblong of paper attached to a wall. He went up to it and when he was nearly there he could see that it had a black arrow drawn on it. He lolloped round the side of the house in the direction in which it pointed. The voices were getting louder. It seemed strange that there were so many here already. His heart drummed inside the nylon costume. He felt laughter bubbling beneath his blank white mask. Then he was in a garden full of scents and murmurings, hazy and soft-edged without his glasses. Dotted around in it, he saw impressionist figures. He was drawn into a little crowd. Things whirled round. The crowds seemed to part before him. He saw a woman tall and black in softest focus, like a black-and-white film star. Melody. The crowds fell back. Behind his mask he was worried. Something was not right. The voices were stopping, except in a glass building where there was still murmuring and the sweetness of violins.

He moved towards her until she came almost into focus: a marble statue shrouded in black. Had she come without her disguise? He looked wildly around at the others. None of their dress was fancy. He stood still on the path. The laughter began as a tiny burble but soon it swept through the crowd like a cold, east wind. He looked into the hollows of her eyes. He pointed his finger at where he thought was her heart. His voice came low. It did not sound like his voice. It sounded like the voice of a cat when it is in a cage being taken to the vet:

'Why have you done this to me?' he spat.

He turned his back on them, then. He tried to run on the gravel in his long shoes. He tripped and crashed to the ground. Someone else laughed. There were other sounds like cooing birds which he knew were sounds of pity. His knees were stinging; his hands hurt where the gravel had cut into them. He had to get back to the taxi. He stumbled and skidded back to the other side of the house where more people were coming, running out to see him, people who had not seen him the first time. He fumbled for his glasses. He saw the tiny black shape of the retreating taxi. He tore off his shoes. He ran again through swirls of people in his yellow socks, hitting out and jabbing with his hands. He heard himself weeping. He ran across the grass to the darkness of the woods, the darkness where he knew he belonged.

66

FITCH

Fitch and Pete leaned over the wall and watched Boase stumbling towards the woods. Fitch felt uneasy. Everyone was laughing but there was something terrifying about what had just happened and they all knew it.

'I can't believe he fell for it,' Fitch said.

'Hook, line and sinker.'

'What the hell did she say in the letter?'

'It was a coded message. You'll have to ask her.'

They looked over at the girls. Suzy, Pauline and Lou were sitting on the grass admiring each other's outfits, already forgetting, laughter fading from them. They'd found a patch of grass that was perhaps strictly speaking behind one of the Keep Out ropes but it was an adult-free zone. Fitch went over and asked her. The girls made room for him.

'It's just some stupid song. The one that always gets played when people choose "Heartbreak Hotel" on the jukebox in The Crown. We were in the bar.' She looked down and then up through her lashes. 'Me and Pete were in the bar after school and he comes in and orders a pint as cool as you please and the jukebox gets stuck on that record as per usual apparently and I just had an idea.'

'What's the song?' asked Fitch in disbelief.

'It's called "Send in the Clowns".'

'Never heard of it.'

'Well it goes on about isn't it rich, aren't we a pair and stuff. I just used the words of the song in the letter. And he bought it. Plus some other stuff.'

'What other stuff?'

'Oh, I don't know. I can't remember now. Oh, I sprayed it with her perfume because I happened to have a free sample from a magazine and I imitated her handwriting, obviously.'

'We knew he'd fallen for it because of seeing him going berserk in the memorial gardens,' said Pete coming up behind them.

'What a twat.'

'I know, it's unbelievable.'

All the time they had been talking, Suzy's knee had been touching his. Fitch felt breathless. He tried moving his knee away but she just moved her knee closer so it was still touching his. He kept thinking about what she'd done, standing on the crazy paving outside her house. It was like a promise. He looked over at Pete but he had moved off and was chatting to Lou.

Then someone said the music in the tent was starting and so they moved en masse towards what sounded like the drum and bass inside his heart. As they walked through the kitchen garden, he found Suzy by his side. He turned and looked at Pauline and Lou following behind. They knew what she was doing to him. He could see it in their slanted, mascaraed eyes. He couldn't tell what they thought about it. Their mouths were sealed like glossy buds. It was getting too dark to tell what anyone was thinking. They went inside the marquee. It felt humid and there was the smell of bruised grass and dirty canvas, like when he went to the circus once on Illerwick Green when he was about eight. There was no one else there. They went and hung around the DJ and made millions of requests that he was unable to comply with. No one was actually dancing. It was like a big open stage and everything was exaggerated in the half-light. The bodies made strange shapes on the canvas like shadow puppets. Everyone was watching everyone else. There was nowhere to go to escape. Perhaps he should talk to Pete. The idea appalled him. People sat around on the bales of straw that had been lined up around the sides and waited. Fitch watched Pete. He never seemed to go near Suzy. He was getting tipsy and joking around. There was no animosity in his face at all. More people, old and young, were discovering the tent, ducking down under the flap of the entrance. Someone old started dancing and then they all did.

Suzy's body looked strong and supple as it moved under the lights. His own body felt light and his head was floating. He wondered if this is what it felt like when you took Ecstasy. She pretended to be just dancing with the girls and then sometimes she turned her body to him, face on. He saw the light flashing on her arms and glinting on the edge of her teeth and on her cheekbone where there was a streak of glitter. He tried to make it look as though he wasn't mesmerised by her. The tent was getting quite full now and the music was louder than before. They kept getting nudged together. She seemed to be touching him deliberately when her hands reached out. He felt her hair whip his cheek.

Then they were thrown together and she whispered in his ear,

'Come on.'

He followed her through a flap in the side of the tent. He hoped his dad wasn't watching. She went and leaned against a Land Rover that was parked outside. He thought, this could even be Pete's father's Land Rover for all I know. He pressed his whole body against her. He smelt the shampoo in her hair mixed with the smell of the tyres and grass. It was suddenly cool after being in the tent but where their bodies touched, the heat from inside when they were dancing was captured. He moved his face towards hers. He opened his mouth into hers. It was like being hungry. Then he pulled away.

She said, 'You're gorgeous.'

He said, 'What about Pete?'

She said, 'There's nothing going on between me and Pete. Never has been.'

'But, I thought . . .'

'Well, you thought wrong.'

Then she slipped her arms under his shirt and he felt the trace of her fingers on his bare skin.

'Fitch?'

'What?'

'I was trying to make you jealous. Pete knew about it. He helped me. Please don't be angry.'

He thought for a few moments. He thought of all the times they'd been together. How he'd only heard they were an item through a rumour. He thought, once again, I have been an idiot.

'I'm not angry,' he said. How could he be angry with her in his arms? He kissed her again. It was easy. He went on kissing her and kissing her until he was aware that there was a small audience. He looked up and the audience cheered.

Pete came and slapped him on the back. 'Well done, mate,' he said, 'I thought I'd never live to see the day.'

Fitch said, 'Bastard.' But he could feel himself smiling all over his face.

He took Suzy by the hand and led her back towards the tent, stopping to kiss her twice on the way for their benefit. He saw his father sitting on a bale of straw. He waved and saw his father give him the thumbs up. He thought, Suzy is my sweetheart.

67
VALENTINA

Patrick did not stay in the bath chair. Every so often, he got out of it and staggered towards the plants, waving his stick and scaring people away from him. He fingered the leaves and sniffed the centres of flowers and got pollen on the end of his nose. Sometimes, he stopped and stared as if trying to recall the way it used to be. He made little exclamations and nodded and shook his head. Leo held one side of the chair and Valentina held the other, bending close to him to hear what he was saying. When he talked about what used to be there, he would shout, 'Ain't that right, young Leo?' over his shoulder. He talked about things that they had never even known about, like an auricula theatre, a dove-cote and a display of prize-winning lilies. Valentina saw his life embedded in the garden. On the south side of the house there was a huge and ancient wisteria.

He said, 'I planted that.'

Later he said, 'Of course, you need a great lot of fellas to do it proper.'

And it was true. It was still a very pale shadow

of what it had been when he had been young and there was a head gardener and a team of others working under him.

Valentina felt as if he had been expecting more, as if he were disappointed, but when the taxi door was being opened for him he took her hands and said, 'You've done well.'

He looked from her face to Leo's and his last words were to Leo himself and she couldn't hear them. She only saw him laugh for a few seconds before the laugh became a violent cough. Leo gave her a haunted look.

When Patrick, with much struggling, wound down the window of the taxi, she wanted to say, 'See you soon!' as she usually did, but that would have been lying so she didn't say anything. For the last few seconds, he looked bereft as if he were thinking that he would never come back but Leo called, 'Come back soon!' and he said, 'Aye, aye.' Valentina thought Patrick looked at her as though he wanted to hear those words from her. The car trundled away and made small wisps of dust come out of the gravel like smoke. From then on, all she could think of was that she was leaving.

It was time for Leo to get back to Melody.

'Got to go,' he said. She watched him hurrying back through the throngs of guests.

She saw Jonathan and Melody springing apart as he approached, Jonathan walking off through the shrubbery. She ran to find him.

She decided to tell Jonathan everything that was in her heart.

He said, 'Yes, I know.'

'Is it so obvious?' she said.

'It's obvious to me.'

'Well, I'm going to London tomorrow, so nothing matters.'

'You at least owe it to Leo to tell him you're leaving.'

'I know.'

'I take it you have never actually told him how you feel?'

'How can I?'

'Life is complicated. Things change. You've changed. Look at you tonight compared with how you looked yesterday. Appearances can be deceptive.'

'Yes.'

'Look at what's happened to me,' he said, blushing.

They went back to the others. She noticed that people were staring at her in her taffeta dress. When they got to the entrance of the tent she saw that Melody and Leo were dancing. They made a strange couple; the perfection and grace of Melody's dancing looked odd next to Leo's wild, gangly movements. But Leo was unaware of this and she smiled at him enjoying the music; at least his timing was impeccable. Melody was playing her part well and did not even look in Jonathan's direction once. Leo caught sight of Valentina and beckoned for her to join them. She shook her head. He said something to Melody and came over.

'Hot!' he said. 'Shall we step outside for some air?' Jonathan slipped from her side.

She nodded and waited for him while he was waylaid by people, obviously remarking on the garden. She saw him nod in her direction as he spoke.

Outside in the air, she said, 'How's it going with Melody?'

He paused. 'Pretty well, I think. Pretty well.' He seemed embarrassed. It was nearly dark, now.

'Good.'

They were walking further and further away from the party. Valentina noticed they had gone round two of the Keep Out ropes. She put her hand on his arm to slow him down, but as soon as she touched him he caught her hand in his, as though he were catching a fish jumping out of the water. She felt she could tell him anything now. She looked up into his face under the moon.

'Leo. I . . .'

He seemed to freeze. They were opposite each other, almost in each other's arms. Their hands were knotted together.

'Valentina, you confuse me. I . . .'

She took a step towards him.

'Leo.'

Their faces moved closer. She knew he wanted to kiss her.

'You're not a lesbian.'

'I'm not a lesbian.'

Their mouths touched tentatively.

'I can't do this,' he said, wrenching himself free. He stalked away over the grass.

'Leo!' She tried to run after him in the silly shoes.

She took them off. She saw the edges of herself gleaming, before she felt the patter of rain ruining the taffeta dress.

'Leave me alone!' he roared at her.

And she stood alone under the trees and cried.

68

MELODY

The black evening dress had felt cool against her bare skin when she had put it on. She had pulled it on quickly, at the last moment, not thinking, not taking her time. All this was new to her. Now, she could not do anything slowly.

She had held onto Jonathan's smooth, brown back and said, 'You are my first lover,' and he had said, 'How is that possible?' He had turned and searched her face for answers. She did not know how it was possible. She had said that people found her un-approachable. Now it was different. He had held onto her body and she had placed her cheek against his smooth chest. He was younger than her; it did not matter. She thought, all the time Valentina was leading me to you.

She had said, 'I thought it was Valentina I wanted. Now I only want you.' And he had told her that he wanted her too.

At the party, she saw him always in the corner of her eye. She played out her role with Leo but she thought: Leo does not love me now. She thought: he does not know that Valentina loves him. When she looked at Valentina, she saw her as a little mermaid, as her lover's beautiful twin. She had heard the story of her life and knew that it echoed her own. She smiled at her between other faces and Valentina smiled back. Nothing was as she had imagined. Her world was like a globe tapped by a finger into motion, swirling and shifting the geography of everything she thought she knew. She allowed these shifts to happen.

Boase burst in. She did not laugh. She was distracted. She was keeping Jonathan in the corner of her eye in case he vanished. Boase's face was a shock of white. The rims of his bare, unspectacled eyes were pink like a white rabbit's. His mouth was a tight slit beneath the red painted smile smeared across his face. She did not understand what had happened. She felt the pain of his embarrassment. He pointed at her. Something was her fault. Then he had gone, the crowd folding in behind him, his red sobs spilling into the air. She thought, it is the children; he has been tricked by the children. She looked for them in the gathering dark but they were not there.

She stole moments with Jonathan when Leo left her side. She felt Jonathan come to her, his breath against her cheek. But she was the headmistress and they moved away from the crowds. They held hands surreptitiously in the garden. They avoided the eyes of Illerwick. When people turned their heads at the sight of Jonathan in Gabriel's clothes, they ignored them. They found a gravel path away from other people and walked along it. Soft leaves brushed their faces. The humid air made them want to hold on to each other for support. There was no one looking. They were going down the path to the old tennis courts. They had left the party behind them, far away. Here the air was different, cooler. There was the sound of a light wind. A light pattering of rain. They kissed. They didn't hear footsteps. Here the gravel paths petered out into flattened earth. Melody opened her eyes. She was watching the closed lids of Jonathan's eyes as he kissed her. She saw a figure in the trees. The red spot of a cigarette. A whiff of smoke. Hard breathing that was near and then faded away.

'Who was that?'

'I don't know.' But she did know.

They ran back as the rain got heavier but when they got there the party was ending. Leo was in the orangery saying goodbye to everyone, a cigarette in one hand. Everyone was drunk, not minding about the rain. She went over to him and took his hand in her gloved one. Through the glove she could feel the tension in his fingers. He smiled but she knew that it was not a real smile.

'There are taxis waiting at the front of the house,' he said with infinite politeness.

'Thank you, Leo. It has been a lovely party.'

They walked carefully to the front of the house, squinting in the rain, his hand under her elbow. He made a sign to one of the drivers and a car drew up. He kissed her delicately on both her cheeks.

'Good-night,' he said in a tightly coiled voice.

'Good-night.' She looked into his eyes but they were dark holes. She thought, what have I done?

The taxi picked up Jonathan further along the drive where Leo could not see. They did not speak. When they got back they undressed quickly and lay in the dark, listening to the rain.

Jonathan said, 'Leo will be all right.'

She said, 'What will happen to us?' but he had fallen asleep, his body sloped against her own.

In the morning she rang up Mr Boase but there was no reply. Behind a flowerpot near the front door she found a bedraggled red rose wrapped in cellophane, the words on a little card all washed away by the rain.

69

LEO

The last guests had gone. Leo went into the house and shut the door quietly. He went to the piano and played the opening bars of the *Moonlight Sonata*, then he banged the lid down. Tiny springed noises stayed in the air, like mosquitoes. His face felt tight and strange. His throat was squeezed shut. He climbed the mountain of stairs and went and lay in the room with the hand-painted wallpaper and the embroidered coverlet. It was the room he had wanted to share with her. He saw her in the corner of his mind dancing, dancing on a tennis court that had been unused for thirteen years. She was not real. He knew that now. The room was spinning. It was his whole world changing now, tonight. A revolution.

He got up and stood by the window listening to the rain. It was nearer dawn than midnight but it was still dark. He pressed his hands against the cold glass seeing nothing and no one, except two faces under the moon and the flash of white-skinned arms, like swans' necks, in the depths of the leaves. He thought of the patter of rain sinking into the cloth of his jacket as the realisation of what he had seen had seeped into his mind. He saw Valentina's face tilted up towards his. His mind beat in time to the ticking of the rain on the window. He sat up suddenly. She knew. He fumbled for his cigarette case. It was empty. He went back down into the hall, into the red room and that was where his anger began to flare. He thought: she knew. She has deceived me. It is her brother. They all knew. Tonight they knew. He thought of them conspiring against him, tricking him into thinking that there was hope. He did not care about hope any more, or Melody or anything except that Valentina had betrayed him. He put Rachmaninov on the gramophone player. He sat in the winged chair. He smoked until he could hardly breathe.

70

FITCH

Ten o'clock in the morning and the sun is bright everywhere but Illerwick is groggy after the party. Fitch is on his way to Beech House because he said he'd help clear up. His mind is still full of Suzy. He takes a detour via Brydges Gate. He goes to Number 23. All the children of Illerwick know this is where Boase lives. It is one of the scary places when you are small. The garden is bare. A tarmac drive. A shut-up garage. A minute square of lawn, which is looking rather straggly. Two hanging baskets placed symmetrically on either side of the front door with nothing growing in them. No weeds. No flowers. No anything. The curtains are all drawn. At every window there is a screen of beige-lined mock velvet.

Fitch goes up the path. He stands by the door and thinks of knocking. Around him are the other houses with opened curtains and open windows and a toddler playing on the steps on a tricycle and a dog yapping. He knocks on the frosted glass, full of panic. He doesn't know what he is doing there. He waits and there is enough silence and stillness to hear the gritty wheels of the tricycle, a little boy laughing, the pigeons flapping their wings in the sycamore tree across the road. He taps again but this time only lightly with the tips of his fingers like someone who doesn't want to be heard. He goes back to his bike at the edge of the drive. He turns his head, thinking he might see the flicker of a curtain. Then he cycles off.

In the woods he slows down and walks with his bike by his side. In the woods it smells dank and dark, of the nocturnal animals who must have come out when the party music faded away. He thinks of Boase, caught in the dark, inside a tangled mess of brambles. He sits on the log where he read Miss Vye's note. He wants the feeling of last night still to be there but it's gone. Suzy will be on the motorway by now, going with her grandmother to meet her mum coming back from Spain. But there is tomorrow and the next day and two whole weeks of the summer holiday left to be with her. It is a sweet feeling inside him that makes him smile to himself alone in the wood. Except now there is the worry of Boase. He knows they have done something terrible. He gets up and keeps on going, wheeling his ticking bike through the darkness inside the wood. He thinks of the grotesque face of Boase, the crying, the long yellow socks fleeing desperately across the grass.

When he reaches the lawns, the marquee is already half down. The marquee men are wrapped up in their own particular choreography that must not be interrupted or interfered with. A circle of flattened grass is emerging, the only sign that something happened here last night. Fitch tries to find the exact spot where he kissed her. He is looking for tracks of the Land Rover they leaned against but there are too many tracks of other vehicles now, mashing up the grass. He goes to the orangery and tries to look helpful but the catering company have everything under control, methodically clearing and wiping and emptying things and carrying. Valentina is not there. Leo is not there. There is no one to tell him what to do.

He goes to the stable. He can see its doors are closed but he goes towards it anyway because there is nowhere else to go. But then he hears voices. Arguing voices. He backs off. He doesn't want to hear. He doesn't want to get caught up in any more disasters. He finds himself going back through the wood, back past the smell of badgers and out into the open and into the town again. He goes back home and paces about by the vegetables and thinks about telling his father everything. He knows they will all get into trouble. He knows that Suzy is the one who is really to blame and he wants to step in before she gets it in the neck.

He is outside Boase's house again. Now it is afternoon and there has been no change in the curtain situation. He has a sick feeling. He thinks of the man's face under the make-up. He thinks he'd better get Pete but he knocks one last time, peering through the misty glass in search of shapes and shadows. He waits. He thinks. He thinks, this man will kill us if he finds out the truth. Then there is a crash like fifty school dinner trays being dropped on the floor at once. He jumps. He runs away from the door. He goes back slowly, seeing for the first time that he could have looked through the letterbox all along. He flips it open with the edge of his little finger. Inside there is a neat and empty oblong of beige carpet with manufactured flecks in it, like tiny bits of twigs. The skirting boards are dusty and the doors are all closed.

'Mr Boase?' he calls.

Nothing. Just stillness and the weight of the dark rooms pressing in from all sides. He sits down on the doorstep. He nods at the people passing by who do not seem to think there is anything odd about a boy who sits outside people's front doors and peers through their letterboxes. They smile back and chivvy their children, looking as though their heads are full of nothing.

71
LEO

He woke up with a start, still in the red chair. It was gone ten o'clock. He got up and walked out of the front door. The morning was fresh and dewy. It did not quench his anger. He knocked on the door of the stable. She opened the top half. She looked at him. She opened the bottom half. Everything was very tidy. He shouted. He said that he knew. He knew. He saw them. Why hadn't she told him? He demanded this of her. He went and leaned against the whitewashed wall and folded his arms.

He said, 'I trusted you.' He said it quietly. He looked at her pinched face and the tears pricking in her eyes. He knew that he was being cruel. He carried on.

He said, 'You have betrayed me.' He watched how his voice hurt her. He did not care. He did not stop. He kept saying it.

He said, 'You, the one I trusted most of all. You have deceived me and lied to me.' The violence of his own anger shocked him.

She ran up to the loft. He heard the zipping of

a case. He watched her as she struggled down with it, balanced on her head, panting and shaking.

She stood in the centre of the room. Her face was white.

She said, 'Leo. You have deceived yourself.'

He said, 'Where do you think you are going?' as if he were her lord and master. He felt something draining out of him, like a black liquid pooling on the floor. He could not think clearly. He wanted to rush over to where she was standing, so small. But he could not. He could not just suddenly do this. He could not admit anything. He needed time.

He said, 'Don't go.' It came out like an order. He went towards her. He put his hand against the side of her face, cupping the shell of her ear, gently.

She said, 'Don't touch me.'

She took him by the wrist and threw his hand back to him like poisonous hogweed. He thought, now I have lost her. She sat on her case and folded her arms as if her train were departing from a platform right there in the stable.

He said, 'At least let me take you to the station.'

She said, 'Don't be ridiculous.' She took a card out of her pocket. She went over to the telephone and picked up the receiver.

He felt a surge of anger again, boiling red inside his chest. '*Did* you know?'

'Know what?' She was still. Her eyes focused on him, suddenly clear and sharp.

'About them.'

She shouted, 'Leo, it has nothing to do with them!

She has never loved you. Accept it. I was only trying to stop you from breaking your heart.'

He tried to speak and made strange sounds. He ran across the yard. He ran into the cold house. He went into his room and buried himself under blankets and tried to shut out the sound of her taxi on the gravel drive. He stayed there until nightfall, then he got up and blundered about in the garden, realising everything.

72
FITCH

He tries again.

'Mr Boase. Are you all right?'

He hears a dragging noise, then a series of soft sounds that seem like his own breaths until he notices yellow-socked feet slowly descending the stairs. Gradually the man is revealed. Pyjamaed. Dressing-gowned. Crumpled. All traces of make-up scrubbed from his gaunt face. He does not open the door. He stands behind it like a terrible stain.

He says, 'Bugger off.' His voice is different, his words clumsily glued together.

'It's Fitch.'

'Fitch?' There is a pause, time enough for him to have opened the door and lashed out. He laughs in a way that is hardly distinguishable from crying. Fitch thinks last night has driven him mad.

'Well, Fitch, she done me wrong, boy.' Now he sounds like a Country and Western singer, all whiskied out and exhausted with crying.

Fitch stays looking through the letterbox at a patch of navy towelling dressing-gown. He thinks, in these situations, whatever these situations are, you should keep people talking but he can't think of anything to say. What do you talk to Maths teachers about anyway? Pythagoras?

'It's the darkness I can't stand.' Boase's voice is small now.

'Why don't you draw your curtains?'

This seems to be the straw that breaks the camel's back. The shadow of him slumps down to the ground and falls against the wall. Fitch sees an empty bottle of whisky slip from his fingers and bounce off the radiator, miraculously, without smashing. He watches the grey, tufty head bow towards the chest and the way the shoulders shake and the face contorts into a strange yawn-like shape when the tears ooze out. Fitch starts to get up. He is seeing things he should not see.

He says, 'I'd better go.'

He sees the face look up. It does not seem to be able to focus properly.

'No,' Boase says. 'Don't go.'

Fitch releases the flap of the letterbox and leans against the wall of the porch. Only the sheet of patterned glass divides them. He knows he has stopped hating this man. The telephone rings in the background and then stops. Fitch puts his head on his knees and thinks, we have played a trick on Miss Vye as much as him.

The letterbox is pushed out from the inside. Fitch sees the lips at the opening, smells the stench of his breath.

'Wait,' he rasps.

Fitch waits. He hears the sound of shuffling, the

brush of dressing-gown against wall, sees the dark shadow move into the darkness of the house.

After a long time Boase pushes out a sheet of squared paper that looks as though it has been torn from someone's Maths book.

'Give her this,' he says.

Fitch pulls the note from his grasp. He thinks, this is one note I will not read.

He runs towards his bike. He realises that his hands are shaking. He cycles straight to Miss Vye's house, posts the note and goes home. He thinks: we will just have to suffer our punishments.

73

VALENTINA

London is hotter than Illerwick. For eight months it has been roaring on without her, without Jonathan, juggling all the people in its sweaty, grey hands, stirring them up in its swamp of traffic and dirty buildings. The bus surges through the grime and litter and glitter, past the gaudy hoardings by Finsbury Park station. She looks down from the top deck at the people slumped round at the bus stop outside Tesco's. They are used to waiting for buses, to the chaos of the street. They look resigned. Some of them look mad. The shops slide past: the racks of clothes, the second-hand sofas, the meat being unloaded from vans, the slopes of fruit and vegetables, the hairdressers, the pizza parlours and the pubs where old men in hats sit half the day outside on the pavement, not minding the squeal and diesel of buses, just chewing the fat. Last year, the fact of all this life going on was always a marvellous thing. Now it seems like a kind of dying.

A few stops later, she gets off the bus. The flat isn't far from the bus stop but the wheels of her case grate noisily as she drags it over the pavement.

Once, it falls over on to its side in protest. She goes down the familiar street of Edwardian terraced houses, hot and red-faced in the afternoon sun, past the dusty privet hedges, the patio of gnomes, a patch of maize planted in a front garden, the newsagent, the launderette, the little Greek bakery on the corner. Number 67 is nearly at the end of the street, opposite a half-hearted sort of park. It looks just the same. It was bought with their inheritance money and neither she nor Jonathan has ever particularly liked it.

She heaves the case up the front steps, pulls it inside and shuts the door. It smells hot, airless, dusty. She wades through the heaps of junk mail and unpaid bills, thinking everything will probably be cut off. The doors are all closed. She doesn't even open them. She goes to her room which overlooks the railway line and the jungle garden of the basement flat. She pushes open the window in the wake of a train and new, smaller sounds flow in – someone's stereo, a strimmer, the parrots next door, a woman laughing. She looks at her watch. It's five o'clock and she is shaking with tiredness. The room is very dark after the brightness of outside, her green desk lost in the gloom. She falls on to the bed and closes her eyes, seeing herself from loft height the way she lay last night on the chaise longue, her heart splintering slowly into shards. She tells herself: Leo does not love you. This is something which you must accept.

When a hooting train wakes her, the sun is setting spectacularly over the railway line and it is cooler.

She gets up and watches the pink and orange streaks fade from the sky. In her chest is the lead-heavy feeling of her heart already reassembling itself into something ugly and spoiled. Downstairs she hears someone whistling in their kitchen and the television on. Life is carrying on. She thinks of Jonathan, far away now on a different kind of island with Melody.

But life went on for her too. She existed in a kind of bubble, not seeing anyone, not telling anyone she was there. It was a kind of secret life. She embarked on a cleaning venture inside the flat and tidied up and paid the bills with the last of her money from Leo. When she was tired of cleaning, she climbed out of her bedroom window and sat on the flat roof with a plan of re-reading all her favourite books, starting with *Pride and Prejudice*. When it got dark, she climbed inside and sat at her green desk, composing bad poems about Leo which she copied out carefully in black ink and then tore up in disgust.

Once, Jonathan rang up to say he'd decided to stay with Melody for a little longer, but she pretended someone was at the door and put the phone down because the way they had changed places was too strange. She thought of Melody and wished she had been able to talk to her as a friend. She thought of everything she had left behind. The garden unfurled itself like a map in her mind. She made plans to get a job in a bookshop which she never acted upon. She sat up writing in the early hours when Illerwick didn't seem so far away. Only at night, lying in the darkness, did she think about Leo and allow herself to cry.

One day, a large envelope arrived that had been forwarded unopened from Beech House. She recognised the loops and kinks of Leo's writing and crossings out on the front and tried to interpret them as though they were hieroglyphics. Eventually, she opened the envelope. Inside was a letter from a magazine telling her that she had won a competition. There was a copy of the magazine with her story about the Little Mermaid that she had read to Melody printed in it. A cheque fell out on to her toast and marmalade. She had never entered a competition in her life.

74

MELODY

'Mr Boase will be away for quite a while.'

Melody could hardly bear to look at the three pained faces in front of her desk. They had been so stupid. She had been so stupid, not to see what had been going on.

She tried to get rid of the image of what he had looked like when she had gone to his house but it kept rushing into her head like the smell of vomit: his pale, bleary face, trying so hard to tell her something, his fingers on the red stretcher blanket like sticks of chalk as they loaded him into the ambulance.

Suzy started to cry. She said, 'He will be all right, won't he?'

Melody saw Fitch reach out and touch her hand. She guessed that it had been Suzy's idea. Suzy had always been full of ideas, even when she was in the first year.

She stood up. 'I have listened to everything you have told me. I realise that there were things that I was not aware of.' She looked at Pete. 'But you should never have taken matters into your own hands.'

She told them that she was suspending them and that their parents had been told to stop them seeing each other until half-term. She averted her eyes from their misery.

It was the first day of term. She watched them shamble out. She saw the supply teacher she had appointed walking timidly round the edge of the playground, clutching her new mark book to her chest like a shield.

When she got home in the evening, she found Jonathan sitting at her father's old desk looking out of the window at his future. She went over and kissed the back of his neck. He turned and smiled. They had only known each other for three weeks.

'Let's go for a walk,' she said.

And so they walked, hand in hand, out of her gate, over the humpbacked bridge and through the fields towards the castle. The sun was warm on their backs but there was an autumnal feeling in the air; the edges of the leaves on the horse chestnut trees were yellowing a little and there was an indefinable feeling that summer was ending. When they got to the top of the hill near some blackberry bushes she looked into his face and he looked back at hers. Last night he had told her that he loved her.

When Jonathan left, it was suddenly summer again. Everyone was saying it was an Indian summer. She drove him to the station and they made light of saying goodbye. They said they would be seeing each other so soon that it was better not to make a big thing of it. Melody did not even go onto the platform to wave goodbye. She just watched him walk out of the sun through the dark entrance. He turned and she waved once and that was it. But on the way home she pulled into a lay-by and cried because she loved him too and she had never known this feeling before and it overwhelmed her.

When she got back to the vicarage, she returned to the house-clearing she had begun in the summer, in an effort to distract herself. She opened the cupboard under the stairs and found Gabriel's duffel bag. She carried it into the kitchen and put it on the table and then she took the things out one by one. First, she pulled out a battered, round-cornered tin of Old Holborn tobacco. She prised it open but the smell that came out was faded and stale. There wasn't much tobacco in it, but there was a tiny lighter that she remembered him using and a little stack of cigarette papers. She kept thinking of his touch, the way he would have held these things in his hands. She flicked on the lighter and looked at the life of the flame. She found a woollen hat, and a pair of gloves. In the hat, she found a single strand of his hair. She laid it carefully on the bleached pine surface of the table but when she looked again it had disappeared. She thought of him bare headed in the wind, of his bare hands as he walked along. Then she found his leather wallet. He had gone without all of these things. She knew it was proof that he wanted to die. The wallet was empty, except for a few coins in a little purse section held down by a press-stud. She slipped her finger inside one of the cool flaps of silk-lined leather, feeling guilty, like a lover checking for infidelities, and touched something smooth and square. She pulled it out with her nail. It was a passport sized photograph, black and white. The two faces were pressed together hard, cheek to cheek, crammed into the frame, the smiles wide and manic. Melody found herself smiling back, looking into the two pairs of black eyes. Where had it come from? She had never seen it before. The duffel bag felt empty now. She turned it upside down and one of his pills pattered on to the table. Something else flew out and landed on the floor underneath a chair. She crouched down and saw that it was an envelope. When she saw her name on the front, she sat down where she was on the rag rug and felt suddenly cold and sick. She opened it and read it. Then she sat for a long time with the note in her lap, her mind going back through the things she had not seen the first time round.

75
LEO

October. Leo slowly climbed the stone spiral of steps up to the roof of Beech House and stood looking solemnly down on the map of countryside with Illerwick in the middle. He felt cold air on his face. He saw light glancing off the still green, moving leaves and on the tops of the hills, making them seem round and velvety. In the fields near the river the brown cattle clustered softly under the trees. Huge, arctic-looking clouds were building to the west like banks of snow. He shivered. On his way back through the house he fetched his coat and his grandfather's stick, even though he knew it probably looked affected in a man of his age. The garden was full of spiders' webs and everything was ending. A few bees bumbled on incongruously in corners and in the depths of the borders he heard robins sweetly marking out their territory. 'I must carry on the work in the garden,' he said to himself as he skirted the lily pond. But he found that, now, whenever he went into the garden, he was holding his breath and not stopping to look at anything, like someone swimming under water. Fitch did not come to work there any more, although he still came for his piano lessons. Apart from Fitch, and Ellie, who came once a week to do the hoovering, he saw no one else. Eventually, he had been driven back to the manuscript of his instruments book out of sheer loneliness and had been surprised when it had begun to take shape at last.

Now he was going to see Melody. He was going to see her because she had asked him to. And, because he was cured of what he now thought of as 'his infatuation', he had agreed. He had put down the telephone and gone to the roof and breathed the air. He had thought, perhaps now we will become friends, if that is not too ludicrous. In the beech wood, a few fallen leaves skittered about but the hard frosts were yet to come. He knew that all it would take would be a cold snap and a windy, rainy day and then all the leaves would come down and it would be winter. Already, as he reached the town's main street, he could smell wood smoke coming from the chimneys of the little grey houses. It was the smell of another century, a century in which he felt he would have belonged.

When Melody opened the door he could see that something had happened. He followed her inside the house. It seemed stark and empty, the few pieces of old furniture out of place against the newly painted walls. The door to the garden was open and the room felt uncomfortably chilly. It was like a room made out of snow. He sat down on a rather saggy sofa. In the distance at the end of the garden the willow tree was completely yellow. She was standing before him, holding something in her hand but she seemed reluctant to give it to him. She seemed about to speak and then she stopped herself. She took it back and held it against her chest, then she held it out again and he saw that it was a letter, out of its envelope.

She said, 'It was in his duffel bag. I didn't know what to do.'

He took the piece of paper and unfolded it. He looked at the words. They were words he had never thought could exist side by side. He noticed the writing, the gentle curls of Gabriel's pen. He looked up at Melody.

She said, 'It was you, Leo. He loved you. All along he was in love with you.'

A tiny shaking that had started in Leo's knee was spreading throughout his body. He saw Gabriel's face, as he always saw it, coming towards him across a summer lawn, carefree and full of what he now knew was love. For years he had been unable quite to read that expression. Now he could. His chest began to hurt. He looked at Melody. He saw that she did not hate him.

She said, 'It isn't your fault.'

They both stared out at the garden.

'It was a matter of life and death and I didn't even see it,' Leo said.

'No one did. He was ill.'

'But I should have realised. I should have known.'

She went and sat next to him on the sofa. Gabriel was all around them in the room. She showed him the little photograph. Leo held it in his large hands and looked at himself and at Gabriel. Tears dropped on to his hands. He wiped them away on his coat. He felt Melody's arm around his shoulders. They stayed like that for a long time, then he got up and walked out into the garden. He thought, I think that I see things but then it turns out that I have not seen anything at all. I am just blundering around in a darkness of my own making. He had a vision of himself in the garden the night Valentina left. He thought, will I ever learn?

When he was leaving Melody, it was hard to know what to say. Nothing could ever be the same. At the front door, Melody remembered something and told him to wait. She reappeared and pushed a magazine into his hand.

'There's this, as well. I sent in her story without telling her. Take it.'

Leo didn't realise what it was at first. He was in a daze. He rolled it up and shoved it in his pocket and it was only when he was walking through the beech wood that he got it out and looked at the front cover. It was some sort of literary magazine. He flicked through it as he walked along. And there in its centre pages he saw Valentina's name. He stood stock still in the wood.

76

FITCH

When Fitch arrived for his piano lesson, he let himself in as he usually did now and waved across the hall to Ellie, who didn't turn the hoover off but smiled at him indulgently. He went into the drawing room but Leo was not there. This was the first time this had happened. He stood for a few moments in the ornate grandeur of the room, wondering if he should just start practising some scales or arpeggios. He had something very important to tell Leo. He walked over to the piano and played middle C with the loud pedal down and listened to its reverberations as though it was a special signal that would summon Leo from wherever he was in the house. Nothing happened so he went over to the harp and plucked a few strings, which was something he had always wanted to do but had never dared. He looked at his watch. He had been a little late and now it was nearly ten minutes into the lesson. He thought maybe he should go and ask Ellie if she knew where he was, although surely she would have said something if Leo was out? He returned to the hall but she was starting on the stairs. He went up to the door of the room where he had first met Leo and knocked on the door. The gramophone was playing as it had then. He recognised Beethoven's *Emperor Concerto*. The red chair was empty and the music and the desertedness made it ghostly. He was turning to go when he noticed that Leo was there all the time, sprawled on the floor amidst a pile of screwed-up paper. He looked distraught.

'Oh, hello, Fitch,' he said gloomily, 'is it time already? Sorry. I was in the middle of all this.'

'What are you doing?'

Leo didn't reply. He was immersed again in his sheet of paper, his pen held up to his cheek. He seemed to be racking his brains but finding nothing there.

'Leo?'

'Oh, just writing a letter. Trying to.' He stared into space for a few seconds.

'Fitch?'

'Yes?'

'Can I tell you something?' He looked upset. And then he went and sat in the chair and said that Gabriel Vye had been in love with him and that he had had no idea.

Fitch was silent. He thought how bad things must have to get for you to stop caring about all the people who would be devastated by your death. Could harbouring love inside you and never telling anyone about it make you feel as bad as that? Leo told Fitch what had happened with Valentina.

'I have not so much been blind,' he said, 'as refused to see what was there.'

Fitch thought of how it had been with Suzy and understood what he meant. He thought, I must tell him now.

'I do love her, Fitch, and I know now that she loved me. What happened to Gabriel has made me realise some things. I want to tell her but I just can't seem to write it down in a letter.'

Fitch tried to speak but Leo was caught up in what he was saying. Now he was holding up a grey magazine and saying, 'I so much want to tell her that I admire her story. Did you know? Look, she's in here. She has won this competition. She didn't even enter it. Melody sent in her story without telling her.'

'Wow!' said Fitch, politely. He reached out to take the magazine. He had butterflies in his stomach at the thought of what he was about to say.

'Go on,' said Leo. 'Borrow it.'

'Leo, she's in Illerwick. I just saw her talking to her brother and Miss Vye outside Miss Vye's house.'

Leo was on his feet. He said, 'Lesson cancelled.' He sprang out of the chair and was gone. A few moments later, Fitch saw him dart past the french windows.

Fitch left the house and wandered in the garden. Now he would have time to see Suzy. Ever since the ban, they had been meeting secretly in the summerhouse. There was no way that they were going to be kept apart now, however wrong they'd been to trick Boase. So far, Leo had not noticed anything. Suzy said she'd heard a rumour that Boase was an alcoholic and that he had gone to dry out.

They imagined him hanging on a line like a kipper. But it wasn't funny any more. It was just weird. They hadn't expected him back at school for ages, if ever. But one day last week, he had come back. He seemed more or less the same. He looked more or less the same. He looked through Pete, Fitch and Suzy as though they were perfectly innocent. Fitch wondered if he knew everything now, or if Miss Vye had somehow tried to protect him from the truth. He hadn't told anyone off so far, but then no one messed around in his lessons any more because they all knew. Suzy said she felt sorry for him now. Fitch said his dad had told him that Boase was a braver man than most, which he sort of understood.

77

VALENTINA

Valentina walked towards the beech woods.

She had not planned to come to Illerwick. But one morning she had woken up and listened to the trains going by and thought, I did deceive Leo. I did not tell him that I loved him. And, within an hour, she was at the station buying her ticket. Jonathan was back in Illerwick already, his return to London having been short-lived. He had said life without Melody had no meaning and that he was going to become a teacher so they could travel the world together in their long summer holidays.

Valentina wanted to see Melody too. At first, she had been outraged that Melody had interfered with her life. Then she had realised that she wanted to thank her. Now the idea of being a writer was something real. She had got on the train with that part of the trip planned. She would find Melody and Jonathan. She would thank Melody for sending her story in to the competition. But she had not planned that Melody would tell her that Gabriel had left a suicide note or what the note had said.

She had needed time to think about these things.

She had walked up to the castle alone. She had sat on the grass surrounded by blackberry bushes. She had thought, people do die because of love and they do break their hearts.

She walked now, towards the wood. She was going in the direction of Beech House but she had not thought what she was going to say to Leo. Her mind refused to imagine what it would be like to see him again. Her mind was tired of imagining. It just wanted to wait and see what would happen. Outside the wood, the sky was bright blue and the edges of the leaves were yellow. But inside the wood the leaves were still very green and the thick canopy made it dark. The path through the centre was like a tunnel through the criss-crossing web of branches. Suddenly, she wanted to get out, to escape the darkness and the closeness of leaves and she began to run. The ground was springy underfoot. She felt exhilarated. She had a purpose. She was a writer.

She ran towards the light. She saw Leo standing under an arch of green. She saw him see her smile and smile back. She watched him slowly lift his arms out and hold them to his sides. He looked like a beautiful tree. She ran inside his arms. She felt them make a circle around her.

78

FITCH

December. Fitch was walking through the grounds of Beech House after his piano lesson when he felt the first few flakes of snow. He stopped where he was, in the garden that had once seemed like a garden in a dream. He remembered the garden on that day in autumn when Valentina came back and he and Suzy had crept from the summerhouse through the laurel bushes. He remembered how Suzy had held up her finger and he had fallen silent at her command. How they had seen Valentina and Leo smelling the last rose of summer each in turn. How they had watched them kiss and then walk down the path hand in hand. For all his life, when anyone talked about love, he always thought of that moment.

ACKNOWLEDGEMENTS

I would like to thank my editors, Alison Samuel and Poppy Hampson, and my agent, Caroline Dawnay.

I would also like to thank Sue Gee for all her encouragement.

And I would especially like to thank my mother for giving me so much always.

CREDITS

'Ain't Misbehavin'' written by Razaf, Waller and Brooks. Used by kind permission of Memory Lane Music/EMI Music.

Lines from 'Silver' by Walter de la Mare. Thanks to the Literary Trustees of Walter de la Mare and the Society of Authors as their representative.

Lines from 'Sea-Fever', by John Masefield. Thanks to the Society of Authors as the Literary Representative of the Estate of John Masefield.